GU01246858

The Importance Of Drinking Tea

by

Rod Hacking

A version of this book appeared in Kindle under the title *Happenings*

To Muriel, Stephanie and Paul
and their wonderful families

A Christian Education

Billy had been in after-school detention – and not for the first time. There was another boy waiting at the bus stop who had been attending a meeting of some club or other. 'I hate fuckin' school,' said Billy, and the other replied, 'From what I hear, the school's not all that keen on you either. You're always in detention. I don't know why you came here.'

'I'll tell you why,' said Billy, 'because my fuckin' mother made me. I never wanted to come to this shit-hole, but she put me in for the entrance exam a year early, when I was still only nine, and when I started I was loads younger than everybody else in the year. I never stood a chance.'

The other boy was clearly shocked by the way Billy spoke about his mother and said, 'I imagine she thought she was doing the best for you.'

'If she was doing the best for anyone, it would be for herself. She told me I was going to be a doctor. She told me, ordered me. Who the fuck wants to be a doctor?'

There was no sign of the bus.

The boy asked Billy, 'Is it true you only got 9% in your end of term Latin exam?'

'What if it is? It's a stupid bloody subject anyway — it's a dead language for dead people. Have you never seen Dr Brill, the head of Classics? I'm sure there's stiffs at the undertaker's with more life in them.'

At last the bus appeared. Billy went on first and immediately ran up the stairs, the other boy went downstairs — he'd had quite enough of Billy Flood.

It was at the beginning of the new term that the bullying began. Being that much younger and smaller than his peers he was an easy and obvious target. Billy realised that the prefects clearly didn't give a toss, nor the masters, who must have known it was going on. Sometimes Billy had to struggle to hold back the tears, but he was determined not to let the bastards have the satisfaction of seeing him cry. There was no one to tell. Certainly not his parents who wouldn't be interested in any case and he had no friends at school (nor out of it, if truth be told). What really got him was the official line that theirs was a caring independent christian grammar school pursuing excellence, measured by the number of Oxbridge entrants each year, and it was already clear to them that Billy would never be among them – so he didn't count. There was no mention of bullying as one of the attractions of the place in the school prospectus, he noticed.

'Never forget that this is a great Christian foundation,' said the Head one morning in assembly. 'Coming here to work in a school with such a strong Christian tradition was the greatest draw when I applied to be your Head. For me being a Christian is the most wonderful part of my life and I very much hope it will be for you too,' and picking up a book in front of him held it high, 'and this is our rulebook: God's Word to the world, and by it we are judged. So remember, you have standards to live up to, the highest, and in later life you will have every opportunity to bring those standards to bear on all that you do. What an honour it will be.'

As they left the assembly hall, Billy turned to the boy on his right and muttered, 'What a load of shit.' The boy looked at him as they walked to their next class and said, 'You're pretty much a load of shit yourself, Flood. This is a great school and we all of us wonder why we have to put up with the likes of you in it.'

One Sunday lunchtime, after his parents had returned from church, his mother said to him, 'You'll be starting Confirmation Class at half past two this afternoon at the vicarage.'

'But I don't want to be confirmed,' replied Billy.

'You are so ungrateful, bearing in mind all we do for you, you horrid little boy. You will go this afternoon, and there's an end to it.'

Billy was beginning to work out that religion really must be bizarre if it was practiced by his awful parents and his awful school. As it was the confirmation classes had girls as well as boys and although the vicar talked drivel, the other sex were a definite attraction, though he was so sufficiently scared by them that he never dared speak to one.

At the confirmation service itself, Billy was seated next to a girl who seemed friendly. When a sweet old man appeared wearing strange, almost fancy, dress, she said to him, 'That's the bishop.'

'Jesus!' said Billy a little too loudly.

'No,' she replied, giggling, 'but close.'

Home had never been a happy or a safe place. From a very early age his parents had often left him alone in the house while they went out for the evening and he fantasised that they might have a car crash on the way home and be killed. They fought one another with regularity, often shouting and yelling. One evening from bed he could hear them rowing again and so loud that he could hear every word. This one was all to do with the fact that his mother had somehow or other discovered that his father had been having it off with another woman. Billy was not surprised and didn't altogether blame him. After all, who in their right mind would want to touch his mother? The thought made him want to puke, but he did find himself wondering whether they might now split up, allowing for the possibility that he might go and live with his father and the new woman and get as far away as possible from his mother. He may not have liked his father, but he was definitely preferable to her. Nothing came of it, and he presumed it wasn't the first time anyway.

School did not improve as the first year drifted into the second. His summer exam results had shown a marginal improvement, but no more. His parents never looked at his school reports and never knew how he was doing. They were still together – somehow, but one night whilst his father was away on business, he heard a man's voice he did not recognise coming from downstairs, and making his way quietly to the top of the stairs he could see into the lounge through the glass partition from the hall. On the sofa his mother was having sex with a man Billy did not know. It didn't actually look much fun and they were moaning and groaning which suggested to Billy that they couldn't possibly be enjoying it. Slowly he made his way back to bed. There was no one to talk to about it and in any case what would he say? He could hardly say anything to his dad, because his dad had done the same, and probably still did. Billy was under no illusions about them. He decided to say nothing, but to store it in his memory bank until it became useful and he was sure it would.

Billy's behaviour at school worsened, and he twice received the cane from the deputy-head for not doing homework on time, his teachers despairing of him. His total contempt for the institution increased almost by the day and he seriously thought of returning at night and setting fire to the place. School was shit, and home worse than shit.

One evening when he came home from school, his mother was in a particularly belligerent frame of mind. 'Go and do your homework,' she ordered.

'I did it in the library at school,' lied Billy.

She was in full flow. 'We are spending a lot of money on you and you're utterly ungrateful. You'll never know the sacrifices we've had to make so that you can go to that school and become a doctor.'

'I've told you before I don't want to be a doctor,' said Billy angrily.

She hit him hard across the face. 'Don't you dare say that.'

'You only want me to be a doctor so you can show off about it — the same reason you sent me to that school in the first place.' Billy left the room and went upstairs, slammed his door closed and seethed with anger and hatred. At least he could get his own back by failing at everything and totally screwing up at school. That would repay her! A doctor? With what he was doing at school he might just make a hospital porter, if she was lucky!

He started skipping lessons and, later, bunking off whole days, often spending days joyriding on trains. No one ever noticed or if they did, didn't care, no doubt preferring his absence to his presence.

Joining the CCF – the school Combined Cadet Force — was compulsory, and Billy hated the fact that on one day of each week he had to travel to school on the bus wearing a military uniform and spend the afternoon engaging in pointless drill in the schoolyard. As far as he could see it simply provided another opportunity for bullying by the NCOs. The only good thing about it, was his discovery that he had a superb eye and was an outstanding shot in the school shooting range and quickly earned himself a Marksman badge.

'Think you're so fucking clever don't you, Flood, shooting those .22s.? Any twat can do that as you've proved. Just wait till we go on manoeuvres and have to fire real guns, .303s with a real kickback. We'll see then what a tosser you are.'

Billy was dreading manoeuvres because he suspected he was in for a lot of bullying by the senior boys who were NCOs, and when the time came he was not wrong. On the range however, firing the big heavy guns, he won the shooting competition easily, though not a single person, boys or teachers, congratulated him. For Billy the very worst day of the year in the CCF was when they marched up through the town as if they were real soldiers to the Parish Church where a nonsensical service was held for Founders Day.

For some time, Billy had had a Saturday job, having seen an advert in the local paper. It was working in the kennels of the local fox hunt. It didn't pay well but he was out in the open air most of the time. He was not involved in the hunting, but helped Arthur the kennelman with his work of feeding, mucking out and exercising the pack of hounds. Farmers and others sent sick and dead animals to the kennels where they were skinned by Ray, the professional huntsman, who was in charge. Sometimes they had to shoot an animal with a humane killer, a sort of gun, and Billy remembered, long after the experience, seeing his first horse shot through the head. Later Ray taught him how to skin, and very often in the winter months, whilst the rest went hunting, he would stay behind and deal with the sheep, cattle and horses that had been brought in. It was a smelly place with no shortage of rats but Billy didn't care. Here he was taken seriously and respected for what he was able to do. Sometimes, after he had finished his skinning and feeding the hot bitches, and hosing down their yard, he would go out with a couple of the older terriers that hadn't been taken out hunting, and would wander through the nearby woods feeling totally at peace.

When the time came to do his O-levels he only just decided to turn up. He had done hardly any work and assumed he would mostly fail, save perhaps in English literature which, strangely, was the only subject he enjoyed. On the day the results came out, towards the end of August, he went into school expecting nothing.

'Who did you pay, Flood?' said the master with the results before him.

Billy took no notice though he wanted to spit in his face. It turned out that he had passed 7 out of 8, mostly at grade 6 which was the lowest pass grade, but he was delighted to see that he achieved grade 2 in English literature. He also smiled and enjoyed the fact that the one exam he had failed was Religious Knowledge. He had at least won one battle for there was no way he could become a doctor with these grades. The school did not ask him, and he did not want, to stay on into the sixth form.

That evening, when Billy returned home, his parents asked him nothing about his results. Instead they wanted to talk about moving house. His father wanted to start a new business on the other side of the country, so they would be leaving here. It was all about them, as usual, and Billy had reached the end.

'I hope it works out for you,' he said. 'But I won't be coming.'

'Of course you will,' said his mother. 'In fact we've already arranged for you to go into the sixth form at a private school, or I think they call it a public school, near where we shall be living.'

'Really?' said Billy. 'Thanks for talking it over with me, as usual, but I'm not coming and that's an end to it.'

'Just how do you think you're going to manage without anywhere to live and without any money because we won't support you.'

Billy turned to face her. 'I wasn't aware that you have ever supported me. The only time I ever saw you supporting anyone was that night I saw you from the top of the stairs screwing someone on the sofa.' Billy got up and walked out of the room, leaving behind him a powerful silence.

It so happened that Billy was quite confident about his position in saying that he would stay behind, following a conversation he had had with Ray at the kennels a couple of weeks earlier.

'Are you really set on leaving school, Billy?' asked Ray as they worked together skinning a cow, which in the heat of a summer's day stank to high heaven.

'No question.'

'What will your folks say?.

'They gave up their right to have a say a

long time ago and frankly I couldn't give a shit.'

'It's just that Arthur's given in his notice. He's getting a bit long in the tooth and if he'd been a hound I'd have shot him years ago. He and Jessie have moved out of the cottage to a new place in the village. If you want the job, and you want the cottage, it's yours.'

Billy believed his luck was changing at last. He could take the hounds out by himself up the lane for exercise – he knew them all by name and they were obedient. Foxhounds are big but usually very soft, and he never had trouble with them. Towards the end of August, shortly before hunting began again, Ray arrived home with the horse box carrying a large tup with impressive horns. He and Billy manoeuvred the tup into the hound yard. The hounds congregated together clearly terrified of this enormous creature before them, which was the point. Ray and he stayed with them, whips ready if a hound so much as looked at the tup, but mostly the whips were not needed. For three or four days they did this for an hour so that when they were hunting hounds would never look twice at a sheep. (Out hunting one day a particular hound was seen chasing sheep. Before the last resort, a bullet, Ray once again borrowed a tup and for five days and nights the hound was secured to the tup by means of a couple – two neck collars joined by a chain. For five days and nights the criminal looked utterly forlorn, but when released never chased a sheep again and indeed would go out of his way to avoid them). Eventually the tup was returned to its home, having other things to attend to in the coming weeks that would certainly demand all his energy!

Anita

That summer, Ray managed to find someone keen to work with horses to help him in the stables and with exercise. She was called Anita and lived in a nearby village. Having been at an all boys school Billy was still shy and uncertain of himself in the presence of girls. Anita was 16 and attended a posh all girls school in the neighbouring town. Weeks could have gone by without them saying a word to each other were it not for Ray's determination that they should, so he made sure that they both came into his house for mid-morning coffee at the same time. Billy discovered that Anita was someone he could get on with, and after a little while, Ray had to end their chatter by chucking them out back to work, and when Anita went back to school in September, only appearing on Saturdays, and even then only for a short time as she used to go hunting, riding Ray's spare horse so he could change halfway through the day, he really missed her.

He managed remarkably well living by himself. He cooked adequate food and bought himself a television. There was a coal fire but no central heating, which of course his parents had had, and he wondered how he would manage in the winter.

Hunting days were long and as the nights began to draw in, much of the work had to be done in the dark. Very early he and Ray would go into the yards and decide which hounds were to go out on that day. Some had injuries and cuts and they had to be excluded. There was a separate yard for bitches in season and they of course would not be going out. Billy would then feed those staying at home and help load up those going out to do what they existed for. In the daytime there was always skinning to do and mucking out and a dozen other tasks. He then had to prepare food for the hounds returning from hunting — they ate an extraordinary amount, their bellies swelling alarmingly. He then had to check every hound for injuries and treat them as necessary, including giving injections of penicillin where appropriate. Finally he had to settle them down for the night on their bed of straw. He called it "reading them a story". Only then was his day over and the evening, or what was left of it, his own.

Very often, after lunch, he would have a brief snooze in his armchair, though on hunting days when he was the only one around, it tended to be a little longer. On this Wednesday his sleep was shattered by a mighty knocking on his back door, which surprised him as it wasn't usually the door people would use. Opening the door, in walked Anita.

' What on earth are you doing here?' asked Billy.

'You sound as if you're not pleased to see me.'

'You know I'm always pleased to see you – it's just that I hadn't expected to see you this afternoon.'

'Well I thought it likely that you'd be here and we're supposed to do hockey on Wednesday afternoon which I very much dislike, so I thought I'd have a heavy period.'

'And how's your period now?'

'"It's getting better all the time" — to quote the Beatles.'

They laughed and chatted for quite a while, before Anita asked Billy, 'Have you ever had a girlfriend?'

'To be perfectly honest Anita, until I met you I never really had any kind of friend.'

'What about Ray?'

'I get on with him perfectly well of course,

but I think of him primarily as my boss, not my friend. What about you? Boyfriends, I mean.'

'A couple, but nothing serious. At my school boys are regarded as creatures from the abyss who will distract us from our work and almost certainly get us pregnant.'

'Chance would be a fine thing,'

'Billy?' . . . 'Do you find me attractive?'

'What sort of question is that?' replied Billy.

'A yes or no sort of question, I suppose.'

Billy waited before answering, wondering whether he dare tell her the truth. 'You are gorgeous, Anita, and I suspect you know it.'

'What matters to me is what you think about me.'

For a brief moment Billy wondered if he had died and gone straight to heaven, before remembering that he didn't believe in it, and was in fact here with Anita in his cottage, which in the circumstances was heaven enough.

'I think you're lovely, but if I'm totally honest I'm also frightened of you.'

'Frightened? What on earth do you mean?'

'I've never had any contact with girls. I don't know what to do or say?'

'Why can't you just be yourself? That's all I want you to be with me.'

Billy could feel himself blushing. The conversation was delighting and scaring him in more or less equal measures. He said, 'Perhaps you won't like me if I'm just being myself.'

'But that's the whole point, I do, very much indeed. When I started coming here it was to ride Ray's horses, and I still enjoy that, but now I come primarily to see you. I'll stop if you want me to.'

'No, no, no. Come every day if you can.'

'I'm not sure my school or my parents would be altogether delighted with that, though I would, and come to think of it, Ray would probably regard me as some sort of distraction from the work he pays you for. In any case, are you planning to stay here forever, cutting up dead animals and looking after hounds?'

'No, this job is temporary but it does give me a house even if it provides me with very little income, but things happen here that I'm uneasy about.'

'Go on,' said Anita intrigued.

'Two weeks ago, before Ray took out the young hounds for their first morning's cub hunting, I saw him go out one afternoon with the working terriers. He was away about two hours and came back with a sack which clearly had something in it. It was a fox cub, not too far off fully grown, but a cub all the same. I was upstairs and he didn't know I could see him. He went to the yard where the young hounds were and then threw the cub, which was clearly still alive, into the middle of them. They did what their instinct told them to do, and clearly Ray wanted them to get the taste and smell of fox before they hunted.'

Anita was clearly shocked by what Billy had

told her. 'Is there more?' she asked.

'Oh yes. As you know last week Carmen had pups. After she had whelped, Ray went into her with a bucket full of water. He picked up each puppy and examined their tails, or sterns, as idiotic hunting people insist on calling them. If any had a curly tail he drowned it there and then in the bucket. I've also seen him, and again when he didn't think I was looking, killing animals in the yard without the use of the gun, using a hammer repeatedly on their head until they drop. Worst of all though, is the way he casually shoots hounds when they get to 7 years old, because he insists they're past their best. He makes me hold them on a lead and I have to lead them out to the muck heap where he shoots them.'

'The rumour in the village,' said Anita, 'is that his wife left him because he used to beat her up. You really have to get away from here, you do know that don't you?'

Before she left, they actually kissed and held each other close.

On her next visit, Anita brought with her a book. 'I know you read a lot so I've brought something special for you to read. It's by DH Lawrence and caused an enormous amount of controversy a few years ago. It's called "Lady Chatterley's Lover". There was a famous trial in London about it. It was supposed to be obscene but the jury disagreed, and I'd like to know what you think about it.'

'How on earth have you got a copy?' asked Billy.

'It's from the school library, though only available to girls in the sixth form. I glanced at it and saw one or two of the more juicier parts, but you read a lot, I know, and I really would value your judgement.'

Billy wouldn't have known the word, but he was actually trying to decipher the "subtext" of what was happening between Anita and himself. He was puzzled and excited.

'You look totally stunning today – in your school uniform.'

'I might look even better out of it.'

'I bet you would, but I've got two calves to skin, and then get the feeding yard ready for when they get back.'

'You're a spoilsport, Billy Flood.'

'Possibly, but I'm totally hooked on you.'

It took Billy a little longer than he had thought to get back to work. Kissing and fondling were just so wonderful.

The horse box arrived back and opening the gate Billy was nearly knocked sideways by the hounds as they made their way to the feeding yard. Once they were done he put them back in their own yard and searched out any who had brought bones in with them – a likely cause of a later fight. He looked out the limping and those who were cut and treated them. He then had to clear out the remains of the raw flesh and hose down the yard.

'They look pretty knackered tonight, Ray,' said Billy to his boss.

'They've gone really well today. It was absolutely cracking. Killed three foxes in the open and dug out another and shot it. Everyone was happy. You should come out with us, you know. If you like, I'll get Anita to give you some riding lessons, but I daresay you'd probably like to ride her. Good looking lass.'

' I don't think I fancy horses. I'm perfectly happy staying here.'

'But do you fancy the lovely Anita?'

Billy was detesting the way Ray was speaking about Anita. This was a man who beat up his wife so much she left him, a violent and cruel man and he was determined not to let the conversation go on any further.

'Anita's my friend and I'm not going to talk about her in that way.'

'Suit yourself.'

Once he'd had something to eat, he decided to make a start on Anita's book. Far from being enticing, he found the early chapters unbelievably dull, and he hoped that when he picked it up again on the following day it would improve. It did, and Billy was left wondering whether in some way this was a coded message from Anita. Did she see herself in some way as the upper-class Connie, and he the gamekeeper Mellors? Was she wanting to re-enact the story? He had found reading the story sexually stimulating in parts but as a story, he did not think it was that good. He had not read any DH Lawrence before, and he wasn't altogether sure that reading this would make him want to read anything more.

On the following Saturday, Ray told Billy that Anita had phoned the kennels to say that she wasn't well and couldn't come out hunting, which meant that Ray had to seek out someone else to ride his second horse.

'This is where you could come in useful,' Ray said to Billy, 'riding my second horse or even learning to be a whipper-in.'

'I'm sure Anita will be well soon. I enjoy doing what I have to. Arthur never rode.'

'Useless piece of shit he was.'

Billy enjoyed working with the hounds, he knew them all by name and they all knew and trusted him. He also realised that part of the job was to help the farming community by relieving them of their fallen and sick stock, but he knew he couldn't take part in anything that, for the sake of what they called sport, involved killing healthy wild animals. He also very much disliked the hunting set. They had come to the kennels in the summer for the puppy show and either ignored or patronised him. He particularly disliked the Joint-Masters, a woman and a man who clearly thought a great deal of themselves. They were his employers and mostly ignored him other than once when they called him by the wrong name and slipped him a £10 note as a tip.

After Ray had set off, Billy got on with his necessary tasks: feeding the hot bitches and attending to the skinning. The meet was on the far edge of the country so he knew that they would be late back – after hunting they all went to a local pub. After washing his hands and arms he would have time to read undisturbed other than for any phone calls from farmers reporting fallen stock which Ray would have to collect on Sunday morning. He went into his kitchen and turned the tap on, the noise of which prevented him hearing the knock on the door, and the first thing he knew about it was the appearance of Anita as she opened the door.

'I hoped you might come,' said Billy, 'and gosh, you're not on your sick-bed.'

'Well . . . perhaps I'll survive if I can get someone to give me artificial respiration. A good long kiss would certainly be a start.'

Billy was more than happy to oblige.

'Ray wasn't very pleased with you pulling out of hunting,' said Billy.

'Ray can go fuck himself. I wanted to be here, alone with you. We both know what sort of person Ray is. You should see the way he eyes me up sometimes.'

'I think you're right. Look, I've just got in from the yards and I'm absolutely desperate for a cup of coffee. D'you want one?'

'Yes please.'

'I don't plan on spending all my life here,'

he said as he made their drink, 'but I've got a house to live in and a job that pays me, but if I had the chance to do something more worthwhile, then I would take it straight away.'

'Would you leave me?'

'I imagine that you'll go off to university and forget all about me, surrounded as you will be by hosts of fit lads. But even if you do that, forget me I mean, I will never, ever, be able to forget you. I think of you all the time. I keep wondering what you're doing and I even find myself envying your school friends. I think what I'm trying to say Anita, is that I think I'm in love with you. I've nothing to compare it with, I'm totally inexperienced, I've never had a girlfriend, never been kissed until we kissed, but I know I love you, and that into what has been for me so far a pretty shitty existence, you've brought something truly wonderful.'

'I feel exactly the same. Lots of girls at school have had much more experience of boyfriends and sex than me. I'm a total beginner but I do know how much I want to be with you. Which reminds me. How are you getting on with Lady Chatterley?'

'Well I've finished it. Do you think he wrote it for effect? Or was it really all about a mining lad having a go at the upper classes? You know, it would be a bit like me writing a story about one of those posh hunting types wanting to have a relationship with me, because I was a bit of rough.

What do you think?'

'First and foremost, and I'm really serious about this, you shouldn't be wasting your efforts here. You should be going to night school and studying A-level English. I know school was hell for you, but this would be totally different – you could even do a second subject, like history. Doing the right subject and in the right place you could do very well at university. Please think about it. . . But what did you think of the sex scenes? Was the court correct when it said they were not obscene?'

Ignoring what Anita had said about night school and university, he replied, 'All I could think of was you, and as for obscene, it strikes me that there are far worse things in this world more obscene than a book showing people enjoying themselves. You and me have grown up with the Vietnam war on our televisions every night – that's what I call obscene.'

Anita suddenly said, 'D'you know, I'm sure we would be much more comfortable upstairs.'

The most Billy could do was to nod his head in mute agreement as she led him by the hand up to his bedroom, where at once she began removing her clothes, Billy shyly doing likewise. Eventually they faced one another.

'Jesus,' said Billy looking at Anita, 'you are phenomenally beautiful.'

'Just look at the size of that,' replied Anita with amazement in her voice.

For beginners that was more or less the

climax, the rest being something of a farce that left them both in fits of laughter. Billy couldn't hold back and Anita was overwhelmed with pain, but she said that next time it would be much easier, and in any case this had been so, so, wonderful. They lay in each other's arms for a long time and hated it when they had to get dressed, and Anita left before the hounds returned.

There was a next time, and many more next times after that, and the effect was to draw them very much closer to one another. One Sunday Billy even joined Anita and her parents, Gerald and Helen, for lunch, which he thought was very brave of him, and them. One thing troubled him however, and the next time they were able to be together he talked to her about it.

'You've never asked me to wear a johnny. Isn't that dangerous?'

'A friend at school told me that her boyfriend said it was like having a bath with your boots on! And that it's nowhere near as good for either of you. I want to feel you totally close, and not a piece of rubber between us. That's why I'm on the pill. When I hoped it might happen, and when I knew I wanted it to happen I went to see the doctor and she agreed.'

'Do your parents know?'

'No way. The shit would really hit the fan if they did.'

They were both due to be 17 that summer and wanted to learn to drive. Anita's father had already begun taking her out on the empty spaces of the trading estate which were empty in the evening. He himself was dependent on Ray teaching him, but Ray had an ulterior motive. Once Billy could drive, he and not Ray could go out and collect fallen stock from the farms. They both passed their tests first time round and Billy's days were now much busier, but at least Anita could take him out in her new car in the evening.

On one such evening Billy was clearly agitated.

'I can tell something is the matter, what is it?' asked Anita.

'That bastard shot Galloper this afternoon.'

'Wasn't he your favourite hound?'

'Yeah, and he made me hold him while he did it.'

'It would have been very quick, he wouldn't have known.'

'I know,' said Billy, 'but it's wrong, and it's the last straw for me. I may have to stay here longer but I'm going to do what you suggested and register for night school, to try and improve myself and get me out of this shit-hole that I've got myself into.'

'We've got a big house. I'm sure mum and dad would let you come and live with us while you did your course.'

'I'm not altogether sure that would be a good idea — are you?'

'Tempting, but maybe not. But what will

you do at night school?'

'Well, English lit of course, and probably History. I been reading quite a bit and I'm interested to know more, to understand why things are as they are. It's really stimulating.'

'Anything else stimulating that I can help you with?'

'I thought you'd never ask. Let's go back to the kennels and I'll make you a cup of coffee or something!'

'Something will be just fine.'

They made love and then she left. That was the last time he saw Anita.

Afterlife

It was Ray who brought the news back from his
visit to the village shop. All he had been told was
that Anita had been taken seriously ill and was in
the Infirmary. Billy at once rang Anita's parents to
find out more details.

      'Hello? Is that Mr Castle? It's Billy here,
Anita's boyfriend, I've heard she's been taken ill.'

      He heard the phone go down with a clatter,
and then Anita's mum picked it up and began a
tirade. 'I don't know how you have the nerve to
call us. You are the cause of all this, no doubt
forcing her to go on the pill when she was just 16
so that you could have sex when you wanted. Now
she's had a deep vein thrombosis and is fighting

for her life – all thanks to you and your total selfishness.'

Billy was already in tears. 'But it really wasn't like that. Anita was already on the pill some time before we ever had. . . intercourse.'

'All this will come out at the inquest if she dies and do not think you will escape scot free. In the meantime do not ever make contact with us again.' She hung up.

Billy wanted to be sick. He told Ray that he was going to the Infirmary and set off at once. On arrival it took him some time to find out which ward she was on – it turned out to be Intensive Care. He rang the bell at the entrance of the ward and a nurse came and opened the door.

'My name is Billy Flood and I've come to see my girlfriend, Anita Castle, who's a patient with you. How is she?'

'I'm afraid she's very poorly, but I can't let you in to see her; her parents have instructed us not to admit you, I'm sorry.'

'They don't know how much we love each other.'

'Probably not, but Anita is under 18 and what they say goes.'

By this time tears were coursing down the cheeks of Billy and he felt a mixture of terror and anger. What would he do without Anita?

'Why don't you go along to the canteen and get yourself a hot drink, and settle yourself before you have to leave.'

'Don't you see how terrible this is? They're preventing me seeing the girl I love, and who loves me.'

The nurse reached out an arm and put it onto his shoulder. 'I know it's wrong, and if I could I would let you in, but I have no choice in the matter. All I can say is, I'm sorry.'

Billy tried a smile through his tears and then turned and went back the way he had come in, all the while wondering how he could possibly go on if she died. She was his life and although they were both so young, they had already talked about a life together in the future.

On the following morning, Ray returned once again from the village where he had been buying a newspaper and some cigarettes. Billy was preparing to take the hounds out for exercise and was already in the yard waiting to release them from the box. He could see it on Ray's face.

'I'm sorry Billy, but the news in the shop was that Anita died last night. They're saying it was a blood clot in the lung.'

Billy was utterly numb, and then said, 'I'll take the hounds up the lane now. I've got just about everything else done apart from a stirk I need to go and pick up from Adams's farm.'

'I'll do it if you like.'

'No, it's all right, it'll give me something to do and I'll probably skin it when I get back, it'll be best if I stay busy.'

He opened the box and a host of large hounds poured out, many of them jumping up, pleased to see him. He spoke a command to them and they stood still and as he set off they walked behind him. It was if it was completely unreal. Here he was getting on with the ordinariness of daily living, and she no longer existed. She was dead. Later, when he went to collect the stirk, he gave serious thought to driving the van at speed into a wall so he could be with her. He noticed a large church as he drove by with a notice proclaiming "Smile - God loves you" and he called out 'What sort of fucking God would do this?', but didn't wait for a reply. The only thing that came was tears, many tears.

Two days later, early-morning tasks completed — feeding, mucking out and exercising – Billy returned to the cottage to make himself a drink. He had not been long inside when there was a knock on the front door. He opened it and to his great surprise saw Anita's mum, Helen.

'I know you won't want to see me, Billy, but please may I come in?'

'Of course. Please come in Mrs Castle and sit here. It was where Anita always sat. Can I get you a drink? Even Anita got used to my coffee eventually.'

'No thanks but please go on with yours.'

'I'm more pleased to see you than you can know, to see anyone who was close to Anita, and not least because you look so much like her, but I imagine that you're here to rub in what you said on the telephone, that I was the cause of Anita's death, and that this will all be made clear and become public at the inquest.'

'No, and to be honest, Billy, when you've heard what I have to say, my only hope can be that you won't throw me out or feed me to the hounds.'

'Not enough meat, I'm afraid, Mrs Castle.' They both smiled.

'Gerald and I have done a terrible thing, for which I do not know if we can ever be forgiven — that's how terrible it is. And if I say the word "sorry" then I do not believe it could ever suffice to express what we feel. It would be utterly and totally inadequate. And if we were not to be forgiven then I truly believe we would deserve it.'

With a puzzled expression, Billy looked intently at Helen.

'The thing is, I have spent the last two days going through Anita's belongings, including her diaries. Perhaps I shouldn't have done so, for they were definitely private, but I am glad that I did. You might well be somewhat embarrassed by some of the things she says about you, often in the kind of detail that made me embarrassed. But I read there something important, something that has made us realise what a terrible thing we have done. As you told us on the phone, and Anita is explicit about this, she went to see her doctor about going on the pill well before you had sexual relations. It was her idea totally, and the only person she had discussed it with was a friend from school, who she reports, thought her a very late arrival on the sexual scene. Her diary is quite explicit, it was her who led you to bed, and not the other way round.'

Helen's face was running with tears.

'Anita loved you very much indeed, Billy, and she wanted for you only good things – to get away from this place, to study and get to university, and she also wanted you to come and live with us. Did you know that?'

'She did say something like that once.'

'Well, we think her diaries rightly belong to you. Perhaps they might go some little way towards making up for the terrible things that we did to you – blaming you and not letting you see Anita while she was in hospital. I'm so, so sorry, Billy, and I can only hope that one day you will be able to forgive us this terrible thing. But for now I want to ask you one thing, that you will come to the funeral and sit with Gerald and me. We three are the most bereaved and we should be together, supporting one another, as I really believe Anita would want us to.'

Billy was stunned. He sat in silence after she had finished, then rose and went to her and hugged her and kissed her cheek.

'This must have cost you a great deal, coming here to say all this,' said Billy. 'You must have a lot of courage and a lot of love to have produced such a wonderful daughter. We really were in love and honestly, the sex was secondary even if wonderful. I know full well that Anita would want me to be close to you, and I want to be close to you because of Anita. The question of forgiveness doesn't arise. What happened is over and done with, and I've already forgotten it. As for the funeral, a large part of me can barely face the thought of being there at all, but if I can do it with you, then I will.' With further hugs, tears and silence, Helen made her way home, saying that she preferred to walk rather than having Billy drive her in the van they collected dead animals in!

In the next few days Billy learned what others have come to know, that work can sometimes help the mind from being completely overwhelmed by the pains of bereavement. Kennel life had to go on regardless of whatever crisis might be happening, no matter how important. It was like farming: animals had to be attended to and cows couldn't wait to be milked just because the farmer was feeling unhappy. He'd heard tell of a sheep farmer who couldn't leave his lambing shed to attend the funeral of his son, and in the farming community of which he was a part not one person thought any the worse of him.

On one of his free afternoons Billy decided to go and see Mr and Mrs Castle. Anita's dad opened the door when they saw him approaching and went out to him and put his arms around him. 'Oh Billy, what have I done? I am so sorry, more than words can express. Please, please forgive me.'

'Mr Castle, as I said to Mrs Castle, that's totally in the past, forgiven and forgotten.'

'We are Gerald and Helen to you.'

Billy smiled and nodded. 'I came to see how you were getting on, and if I'm honest, just to be that much closer to Anita and there's some diaries which Mrs…er, Helen said I could have, but mostly I just wanted to be here with you for a little while.'

Gerald led him into the sitting room, and Helen made them some tea with cake. That was when they dropped the bombshell.

'Anita had often told us, and her diaries confirm it,' said Gerald, 'that you desperately need to get right away from the kennels, and we know that you are doing English and History A-levels at college. Her diaries also describe something of your less than happy upbringing and your estrangement from your parents. If you left the kennels you'd struggle to find somewhere to live, meaning that you're stuck there. That's not a happy situation. Anita said you were very good at your job but that it was a horrible job and that you were caught up in things you hate. Have I got it right?'

'Anita was a brilliant listener. She was the first person in my life to whom I could talk, she was my first and only friend. I told her everything and she knew only too well my feelings about working at the kennels and what goes on there. I was glad enough to go there at the start because there was nowhere else to go. I never go out hunting, but things happen in kennels which I have to see and sometimes participate in, that are wrong, morally wrong.'

Helen said, 'Billy, Anita wanted you to come and live with us, to get away from that place. I rather think it might have caused one or two problems, shall we say?' She smiled. 'Well, we want you to come and live with us now. We feel that it is no less than what we owe you, but the most important reason is that we are absolutely certain that Anita would want it too. And we think you're very special, as she did, and she was a very good judge of character, and we really believe it would help keep Anita's memory alive for us if you could bring yourself to come and live here. You don't have to decide now, but you could be a full-time student here, living with us.'

Billy sat in amazed silence. Eventually he said, 'No decision is necessary. I can't think of anything more wonderful than coming to live here in Anita's house and with her lovely parents.'

Helen left her chair and came over to him at once and held his head close to her.

'Gerald said, 'Thank you Billy, thank you.'

'No, it's me that should be thanking you, and Anita. But you do realise I shall have to work my notice. It really does require two people to do the job there, but I'll tell Ray today and if it's all right with you I'll come as soon as I can.'

As he walked back to the kennels and

thought through everything that had happened he knew he would miss the independence of his cottage and time to grieve for Anita by himself, but he now could be so much nearer his beloved, and well away from Ray and the world of hunting.

Ray was in the stables when he got back, grooming one of the horses and Billy decided to be direct.

'I've decided to leave, Ray, as soon as you can replace me, so I guess this is me handing in my notice.'

'I was going to have to get rid of you anyway. I need support out hunting, not just a kennelman. There's a young Irish lad, whips-in for the Kilkenny, highly spoken of and used to working in kennels. I've had a few chats with him on the phone and I'm sure he'd be ready to come at short notice, so you probably won't have to work very long, maybe just a few days. I'll call him tonight and let you know.'

Billy noticed that Ray had not asked him anything about where he was going to go or what he was going to do. There were no thanks for all he had done. Nothing, and no doubt Ray would soon be speaking of him in the same derogatory way he had done of Arthur.

Anita's funeral would forever remain a blur to Billy. Ray said he couldn't have the day off and whilst he could have the time off to go to the funeral he had first to feed, muck-out and hose down the yards. Afterwards he changed into his suit and walked through the woods to the house. People from the village were already making their way to the church, and relatives flooded the house, not one of whom knew who he was (nor why, feared Billy, that he probably smelled of something not altogether pleasant).

When the hearse arrived Billy could hardly bear to look at it. Did no one but he realise that it contained the dead body of the woman he loved and who loved him? Only Gerald and Helen perhaps, for they were mourning the loss of their own beloved only child. When the time came, Billy was ushered into the first car with them, much to his amazement and the bewilderment of others. Who was he?

In church Billy walked behind the coffin on one side of Helen, Gerald on the other, and was shown into the front pew with them by the oddly jolly-looking funeral director. He never removed his gaze from the coffin and under his breath spoke to Anita throughout, hearing nothing of the vicar's words or prayers. He stood for the hymns but didn't sing, nor did he pray. As they followed the coffin outside he caught a glimpse of the sun breaking through the clouds.

The lowering of the body (the body he had loved and loved still) was too much for him and his tears flowed, this time accompanied by gentle moans. Gerald reached out and put an arm across his shoulder, and when the time came to throw soil onto the coffin now below them, Billy could not do so. Afterwards Billy did not stay long at the funeral tea and deeply resented the fact that so soon after the funeral people were chatting, some even laughing, as they ate their sandwiches and slurped their tea. He knew Helen and Gerald would understand that he had to get back to work, also that for him and them this had been the day in hell they simply wanted over.

On arrival back at kennels Billy saw a car outside with Irish number plates, which must, he assumed, herald the arrival on the Irishman who was replacing him. Going into the main yard, Billy first noticed the carcass of a dead horse which he knew would take him ages to skin and cut up for the flesh house. Then he saw Ray and a red-headed chap talking together. They turned towards Billy.

'Hello, I'm Sean' said the Irishman extending his hand.

Ray said, 'We need you to finish today Billy. We've got hunting tomorrow and I'd like Sean to be out with us. I'll pay you to the end of the month.'

'There's only seven days left,' said Billy.

'Well if you don't want it… and another thing, I'd like you out of the cottage tonight, so Sean can move in. I'm sure he can give you something for the furniture.'

'Of course I can,' said Sean.

'In the meantime, there's still work to be done today. I shot that horse while you were out.

Before you go it needs skinning.'

Nothing else. No words about the funeral or Anita. Nothing.

Billy went first to change out of his suit and to telephone Gerald and Helen, to let them know what had happened and to ask whether it would be possible to come to them today after work.

Billy skinned the horse and took his leave of the hounds, received a pitiful amount from Sean for what he was leaving behind and moved out.

Changes

Soon after Billy had moved in with Gerald and Helen, he received a letter from his father (forwarded from the kennels). He read it and threw it down.

'I've had a letter from my so-called father,' he said to Gerald who was with him when the letter arrived, 'telling me he's getting divorced and that his wife, my mother, has a new fancy man with whom she's going to live in South Africa. He's got a new partner too – there's a surprise — and he's asked me to go and live with them and join him in his business.'

Gerald had a worried look on his face. 'Are

you thinking of doing so?'

He heard the sighs of relief as he spoke. 'I love you two and there is simply no way I would want to be apart from you. I know it's awful in one sense to say it, but I never loved them, ever, even as a small child, and I don't think I could be happier than living our life here together'.

'I know I speak for both of us when I say how much it means to us that you're here.'

Billy read Anita's diaries again and again. Helen had been right, they were extraordinarily explicit, embarrassingly so when he knew Helen had read them. Anita clearly liked explicit detail! He visited her grave every day, and when he had money he bought flowers and took them to her. 'I've brought some flowers for you,' he told her. 'I will always love you, Anita, and how I wish I'd been able to be with you there in hospital, to say goodbye properly and to give you a final kiss, even though our last moments together were exquisite. But it wasn't to be and I don't hold it against your mum and dad. I love being with them and I promise that I will look after them for you.'

Increasingly, he had a sense that they were his parents too.

One evening after his English course at college, his tutor asked him to stay behind. 'If you're going to apply for university, Billy, you need to get your UCCA form done as soon as possible.'

'Ok. What do I have to do?'

'Assuming you want to apply to read English, you need to apply to five universities, and place them in preferred order. I'll write the academic reference. Then you can send it off.'

'That sounds easy enough.'

'Unfortunately there's a minor problem. Your O-level results will mean, I'm afraid, that you'll almost certainly receive five rejections, even though I shall be saying you are predicted A grades in both subjects. However, when the results come in August, you'll be in a very strong position to take advantage of Clearing. You'll sail in then.'

Billy didn't think it just a minor problem and Helen and Gerald were both very disappointed for him, but he passed on to them what his tutor had said about Clearing, and indicated his determination to press on, because he knew that was what Anita had wanted for him.

Anita had told Billy, 'Dad makes curtains'. What she hadn't said was that Gerald *was* "Castle's Curtains", a large firm well-known across the country and probably worth a fortune. It was odd because Gerald was a quiet, unassuming man, not at all how he imagined a big businessman to be, though he did think he was probably very shrewd.

Over their evening meal, Billy said there was something he needed to mention.

'I'm not earning my keep,' he said. 'All I'm doing is studying and living off you.'

'We'd be doing exactly the same for Anita and we want to do it for you too,' said Helen. 'She wanted you to be able to go to university, and we want that too, though only if you want to go.'

'I didn't go,' said Gerald, 'and I've not done too badly, but it seems to be compulsory these days, though the Prime Minister, Mr Wilson, has set up something called the Open University so people can get degrees working from home.

'But there is a matter I want to raise with you. Sitting in the garage out there is a brand new car I bought for Anita when she passed her test. It's pointless it just sitting there, so we'd like to give it you for Christmas, if that's alright with you.'

'I'm speechless. How could I ever thank you?'

'You don't have to,' said Helen. 'You thank us all the time. I've watched you go up to the churchyard every single day without fail. I know how much you loved each other and I think it quite likely that you would have soon been our son-in-law. Well, I already think of you as our son.'

'Thank you, and I feel the same, though if I were your son and Anita was your daughter, that would make for complicated explanations about our relationship, if you see what I mean.'

They all laughed. Billy continued, 'But I mean it. I worked really hard at the kennels and it doesn't feel right that all I'm doing now is studying. I really should have a part-time job.'

'Your exams are very important,' said Gerald, 'but if you really mean it, why not come and work for me two or three days a week? You could come first and see how the business works, and then possibly do a bit of troubleshooting.'

'What's that?'

'All businesses have the occasional problems. Ours are primarily to do with unhappy customers — there aren't many I'm pleased to say, but we pride ourselves on doing all we can to put right what has gone wrong. So we have a number of troubleshooters who go and visit customers and see how we can better bring about customer satisfaction. On the whole it works. I could do with someone working in the southern counties and we could quickly get you up to speed. It's entirely up to you.'

'I like the sound of that.'

'Perhaps we can make a start after Christmas.'

Billy wondered what Anita would say and in the following days he often talked it over with her in the churchyard.

Christmas was inevitably a muted affair, but they tried their best. For Gerald and Helen, however, the most amazing moment for them, was when on Christmas Day, Billy asked them if they would object to his changing his name to theirs?

'I've been to the library and looked it all up. I have to be 21 to complete what they call a "deed poll", but there is no reason, if you are in agreement, that I cannot start using the name Castle with immediate effect. You are the only parents I have ever had, and I would be so proud to bear yours' and Anita's name.'

'That's so wonderful Billy,' said Helen. 'I can't think of a better Christmas present.'

Billy's first and great surprise when he started work with Gerald in the New Year, was that in "Castle's Curtains", there were no curtains.

'The curtains get made in Darlington — we have a big factory there — and from there they go to one of two distribution depots, one for Scotland and the North, the other for Wales and the South. We also have a team of agents who respond to customers' initial enquiries by visiting them on site, taking with them various swatches and then measuring up and dealing with the details of the order. When the curtains are ready, they return and fit them.'

'So what do you do here?' asked a puzzled Billy. 'Somehow I'd envisaged you with scissors and cloth, and a whole host of machinists.'

'That's what we've got in Darlington and I'd like you to go up there and have a look. It's quite impressive and we're able to employ a lot of people in an area of high unemployment.'

'How many people do you employ altogether?'

'That's never easy to say. Machinists leave to have babies and that's not being unkind to women – it's a simple fact of life when you employ so many as we do. Men leave as well, especially drivers, some of whom don't enjoy having to stay away for a night or two. But when you add together everybody, including the telephonists who work here and are the first point of call for customers, it's a lot — over 300.'

'And does the firm have a good reputation?'

'On the whole it does, but it's my job to make sure that continues, by attending to the detail, by listening to people, and hopefully, by making sound decisions.'

In the course of the next couple of weeks Billy visited all the branches of the business. He went by train to Darlington and was greatly impressed by what he saw. He tried to speak to as many of the women that worked there as he could and he was truly impressed by the skills he saw them utilise on their machines though even hounds howling as they waited for their food would have been drowned out by the cacophony of the full canteen. He also visited the Distribution Depots and spoke with drivers. Everyone was very pleasant to him, until he twigged that his new surname would mark him out as family of the boss.

He spent two days with agents and observed as they helped potential customers with design, style and colour, before measuring up. Finally he took the train to Hull where he spent two days with the man doing there what he would himself be doing before long: sorting out when things went wrong. He was offered some unexpected advice.

'Most of the people I have to deal with are

women, and usually women alone in the house. For heaven's sake, don't even think of taking advantage of that situation, and equally, don't let them take advantage of you.'

'You're kidding aren't you?'

'Believe you me I'm not and it almost always leads to trouble. It happens, and it's as well to be warned. Especially a young healthy lad like you.'

'And has it happened to you, that, you know, an offer has been made?'

'Once a fortnight, I would say, and so far I've always managed to resist. So should you.'

The agreement with Gerald was that Billy should work three days a week, leaving the rest of his time for his study and Billy found this a good balance. He enjoyed driving Anita's car and he wasn't at all unhappy in his own company. The job required patience and an ability to express sincere apologies on behalf of the firm when appropriate (however insincere he might have felt personally, given the occasional unpleasantness he encountered). Months went by and not a single offer of a visit to the bedroom had been made. Perhaps there was something wrong with him! Perhaps he needed to change his deodorant! But in all honesty he knew he was relieved.

The end of May brought his exams. He had worked hard and in a way was looking forward to them as an opportunity to show the examiner just how much work he had done. His real problem with the English papers was in choosing the questions to answer because he would have liked to have answered them all. He also enjoyed the History papers. He thought back to his experience of exams at school and shuddered. It had been terrible but at least he was making up for it now.

The exams over, Billy began to work full-time for Gerald, who told him one day that they had had terrific feedback about him from customers. That evening, Helen said, 'We're wanting to arrange a holiday, flying to the island of Ibiza. We went there with Anita and were planning to stay in the same hotel. We'd very much like it if you would come – it's really nice, warm and relaxing.'

'Of course I would. It would be great. But hang on, I can't, I haven't got a passport.'

'H'm. I did wonder, but it's not a problem. You can easily get a Visitor's Passport from the Labour Exchange in town if you take two photos of yourself and your birth certificate. Unfortunately you will have to use the name Flood as it's an official document and can't be changed until you're 21. But we'll know who you are, and you can call yourself Castle whilst you're there.'

'I've never flown before. Isn't it a bit terrifying?'

'No, it's a doddle, you will really enjoy it.

Anita loved flying.'

Later, he went to the churchyard and confessed his fears to Anita, who merely laughed at him.

For Billy, the knowledge that Anita had been here in this place with her parents meant that the holiday hotel was holy ground, and he pictured her in her bikini looking amazing, going in and out of the pool and sunning herself. He swam and read and each evening after dinner sat with Gerald and Helen in the bar and discussed the fascinating Spanish customs around them. There were lots of pretty girls around, many of them scantily dressed in the sun, but Gerald and Helen observed that he did not seem to notice them or ever look twice.

A-level Results Day was a triumph: grade A in each subject, but what to do now? Clearing demanded he move fast, and Billy had been waiting for this day, but he was now hesitant and needed to spend time in the Churchyard with Anita. Slightly frustrated, Helen and Gerald nevertheless did not push him even though they knew that with literally every minute going by, he might be missing an opportunity. He said and did nothing after returning from the grave.

They had booked a celebratory meal at a restaurant in a neighbouring village and ordered champagne.

'I suppose that had other things being equal you would have been celebrating this meal with

Anita,' said Billy.

'That was not lost on me,' said Helen with a deep sigh, 'of course not. But it wasn't to be. What we have come to celebrate is just how clever our son is, to honour your achievement, and what an achievement it is — working for that slave driver Gerald and still getting grade A's. Anita would be furious if we talked about her tonight, and not primarily about you.'

Billy smiled – she looked so much like her daughter, his beloved Anita. 'There are some things I need to say to you this evening. The first, and most important, is to thank you from the bottom of my heart for bringing Anita into this world, and therefore into my life. People in the village probably think, and perhaps even you think, it's either ridiculous or unhealthy that I go to her grave every day and talk to her. As you know, sometimes I stay a very long time, but I need to do it and I know that she will tell me when the time has come to stop. And then I will. Another thing I want to tell you tonight is that I don't think I will ever find the words to thank you enough for taking me in, and loving me, and being such good parents to me, and I want you to know how much I love you.'

By now tears were pouring down the cheeks of both Gerald and Helen and they couldn't reply other than to take hold of Billy's hands and squeeze them.

'The other thing I want to speak about is

what I'm going to do next. The three of us know only too well that life is unpredictable but that shouldn't stop us making plans. So, I've decided not to go ahead with Clearing, and I've almost certainly missed my chance now anyway. I know Anita wanted me to go to university but I'm not ready and I hope she would understand.'

'Of course she would, Billy. She would only want what's best for you, as do we,' said Helen.

'Perhaps you were looking forward to getting rid of me.'

'Probably,' said Gerald with a broad grin across his face, 'but I guess we'll just have to put up with you, hard though it will be.'

'Take no notice of him. I'm totally delighted. It's wonderful news, but do you know what you want to do?'

'I'd like to carry on working for you, Gerald. Much to my surprise I'm really enjoying the job and I'm learning ever such a lot about the manufacture and distribution of curtains. I so enjoyed my visits to all the different places in the company when I started and I honestly feel enthusiastic about what it is we're doing.'

'The job is yours, but we might think of adding to it in a variety of ways. Just give me some time to think about it,' said Gerald.

'I do however want to go on with some study, but not formally, for exams. There's a lot of reading I want to do, to catch up with, that Anita and I discussed and shared. Doing a set course doesn't always lend itself to that. But only if you approve.'

'You have our approval for whatever it is you choose to do, because you are our son,' said Helen, 'and if it means we'll be able to be together, at work and home, then all the better.'

Two days later, Gerald asked Billy if he would cancel his appointments that day, and join him in the office.

'I know we could have discussed this at home, but I felt that here was the right place for it. I've been thinking a lot about what you said the other evening and from the feedback I've been receiving you've been doing really well. In fact, I think you've been doing it so well, the time has come for promotion. I want to ask you to be based here but having special responsibilities for keeping closely in touch with all the out stations. It's not a matter of spying on them, it really isn't, but it's easy to lose touch with the day-to-day realities I can't see. It's not possible for me to be out there and also doing what I have to do here, so I would like you to do that.'

'I don't know what to say, other than that if you think I'm up to it, I will rely on your experience and judgement, and do my best. But I'm very disappointed about one thing. Someone, no names mentioned, told me that in my present job I would find all sorts of ladies at home by themselves wanting to seduce me. It hasn't happened once! And now it never will.'

He grinned.

'I'm so sorry to spoil your chances, Billy, and I bet I can guess which rascal told you that. The irony is that if it ever happened to him, he'd run a mile, and if you'd ever met his wife you'd understand why. I'm sure she is a member of the British wrestling team.'

On his way home Billy bought some flowers and took them straight to the grave. For no reason, and for every reason, he found himself feeling angry about what had happened to Anita and what it meant for her to be dead. As far as he was concerned she would always be alive. Of that he had no doubts, but that did not in any way diminish the anger. He heard footsteps behind him, and turning, he saw it was the vicar on his way home from church, who now stopped and spoke to him.

'You're very faithful. Billy. You and she were very close, I know. Death's a terrible thing.'

'Sometimes I seem more able to cope with it than others. For no obvious reason today I feel really angry. I want to scream and shout and hit something.'

'Well, I'd prefer it if it wasn't me!'

'Does it help if you believe in God?' asked Billy.

'Well I suppose you can always take your anger out on God. Sometimes that helps people but I'm not sure it would for me. I come into contact with a lot of death and a lot of people who, like you, just can't understand why it has happened. You would think that in my job I could handle all that, but I'm very often much affected by it and can easily get depressed.'

'I always thought that religion was supposed to make life wonderful, that it was a way of running away from reality, but what you've said is the exact opposite.'

'Perhaps I'm letting the side down, but it's what I think and feel. And my heart sinks whenever the phone goes and it's the undertaker.'

With a broad smile on his face, Billy said, 'Have you ever thought you're in the wrong job?'

'Yes, often, but I'm not really fit for anything else. A country parish like this is about my limit. Anyway, I'm supposed to be the one ministering to you, not the other way round.'

He made to go and Billy said, 'I'll come with you as far as the vicarage, I'm on my way home.'

Billy enjoyed the new job, especially having the time to listen to those who worked for the firm. He was able to grasp the way in which the system worked and where everyone fitted in, and always looked forward to reporting to Gerald on what he was finding, and occasionally making suggestions of possible improvements, and clearly Gerald was glad that his idea was working well.

Billy had lost the most precious thing he

assumed he was ever likely to know in this world. He didn't know if he was making some sort of recovery and feared he never would, but at least he had found a home, and love, and stability. Nothing could ever make up for the loss he had experienced but he also knew that there was much to be grateful for and he truly was.

Reflections

One morning before heading off to work, Billy made his way to the churchyard to be with Anita. He was discovering what so many others before him have learned, that bereavement and loss are relentless, that days, weeks and months come and go, and nothing changes, the emptiness is always there.

       'Oh, my darling,' he said aloud, 'I know how much you would laugh at my attempts at being a businessman, and you'd probably be cross that I didn't go to university when I had the chance, but I can't leave you, I have to be near you. I'm ashamed to say I've even thought of ending my life so I could truly and finally be with you. It wouldn't be difficult; I know where the skinning knives are kept at the kennels and I could go in when they're out hunting, and it would be very quick. I know exactly how to do it. But, and it's a big but, I just couldn't do it to your mum and dad, and who I think of increasingly as my mum and dad, they'd be utterly devastated again.'

Anita sometimes replied, sometimes not, but always Billy felt restored in some way by the process. On his way back home to collect his car to get to work, Billy bumped into his friend, the vicar, whom, he had discovered, from Helen, was called Hugh.

'Hello Billy, you're up here earlier than usual.'

'A lot to get off my chest.'

'Have you time for a cup of coffee, or have you got to get off to work?'

'I'm the boss's son, well, in effect I am. Who's going to tell me off for being late if I've been visiting his daughter's grave or receiving counsel from a vicar?'

'Coffee it is then. Come on in.'

Hugh showed him into his study which was book-lined and extraordinarily untidy. He arrived with their drinks, immediately apologising for the mess.

'To me it seems lived-in.'

'H'm, I'm not so sure. Perhaps it accurately reflects the state of my own inner chaos.'

'Well if it does, it doesn't show.'

'That's a relief I suppose.'

'I don't think it would do me or anyone else any good to trail my feelings around the place,' said Billy, 'and I've got well used to concealing them. Sometimes it's only in the churchyard that I let them out.'

'I totally agree. Quite often I hate myself for going round with a smile on my face and being cheerful to everyone. I have to do it I suppose. That's what's expected of the vicar but it makes me think that I'm being cheap and denying more of my true self than I can afford to. It's the same at some of the meetings I have to attend, church meetings that is, with other vicars, or even the bishops. They all think that I'm very quiet and must therefore be thoughtful, but they don't realise that if I was to open my mouth and really say what I think, they'd be utterly shocked.'

'I suppose,' said Billy, 'that for you the question is how long you can keep that up. As you may know I used to work in the hunt kennels. I kept my mouth shut about some of the things that I saw and knew were going on, and if I hadn't had Anita to talk to about it all, and she knew a lot of it herself anyway, I think I might have done something very silly eventually. When she died I was able to make my escape. So how are you going to escape from what sounds to me like a trap?'

'The trap you talk about, Billy, is very real. My wife doesn't work because she looks after the children and I'm on a low income because we get given a house while I'm doing the job. If I was to stop doing it, we would have no house and no income, and if I were to say some of the things that I really feel and think, they would stop me doing the job. Unlike some vicars I don't have permanence, what's called the freehold. I can be got rid of and I have no training for anything else.'

'I went to a school that prided itself on its religious foundation and we had regular visits from vicars and bishops to speak on various occasions. If you don't mind me saying so, I thought most of them spoke through their arses. You're the first and only religious professional I have been able to respect and admire. I never thought I might have a vicar as a friend, but that's how I think of you.'

'I really appreciate the things you've just said. I've never told you and maybe she didn't, but I got to know Anita quite well.'

'Seriously? She never said anything to me and there's no mention in her diaries.'

'She came to the vicarage one evening and said she needed some help with understanding the religious situation that underlies Chaucer – it was for her A-level, I think. To be honest I didn't know all that much myself but I tried to find a book or two to help her. Of all people, you don't need me to tell you how special she was — so full of life and laughter, and she was a beautiful girl. I can tell you that if I hadn't already got a lovely wife, and Anita had been a little bit older, you might have had a rival. She told me she wasn't religious at all, which didn't worry me, and she also told me she was in love with someone, though she didn't say who, and that this person was the most wonderful person in the world. It made me feel that whoever that person was, was very, very lucky. And of course, that person was you, and what you have shown me, day by day as you passed my study window on your way into the churchyard, is nothing less than total commitment and love, and it also shows me, what I've been suspecting for some time, is that these most important things need have nothing to do with religion.'

Billy sat in silence for some considerable time, a silence not broken by Hugh. Eventually he looked over to him, and said, 'You're quite right, she was amazing, and we'll never know how she would have used all that she was as she entered the public world. My hope had been that we would do that together, but it wasn't to be. But Hugh, do you ever think I'll be able to come out of this state of total loss and emptiness? Will I ever be able to relate to another woman? Will I ever be able to marry and have children? Or am I completely stuck in my personal tragedy?'

'I could take you to homes in this parish and others, that have experienced horrendous tragedy, notably the death of children. They would recognise your words and feelings, and probably tell you that they will never completely leave you, but they might say that life goes on and has to.

You, Billy, are still newly bereaved and the pain remains acute, but perhaps there will come a day when you notice that it is not quite as bad as it was yesterday. Maybe then you can begin to reconstruct your life.'

As Hugh had suggested, the year went on for Billy day by day and relentlessly. He had his work, but much of the time he thought that all he was doing was pointless. He did enjoy the opportunity to travel and meet his fellow workers, and he was particularly fond of the Darlington factory and its many machinists who really could make him laugh. The manager there expected him to take his lunch with him and the office staff, but Billy loved going into the canteen with the women and engineers. He never minded getting his hands dirty, and when a disapproving word of this got back to Gerald, he was delighted to hear it and gave his full approval, much to the chagrin of the Darlington manager.

Billy arrived home one afternoon after a visit to agents in Wales to find Gerald and Helen in a state.
        'I've found a lump in my breast,' said Helen by way of explanation. 'I saw my doctor straight away, and he's made me an appointment to see a Consultant in the morning at the Infirmary. I think Gerald's in more of a state than me.'
        Billy went to her and gently put his arms

around her, kissed her and said, 'Ok mum, we're gonna get through this'. It was the first he had ever called her that.

In the morning they all confessed to not having slept well, though of the three of them, it was Gerald who most looked like the patient. Billy drove and little was said.

All three were ushered into the Consultant's room, where, behind a screen, he and a nurse examined Helen. When she emerged he said, 'I need you to have some tests done in the X-Ray Department. Being a private patient this won't take too long, and after lunch we will have more of an idea of what we are dealing with and what we need to do. Nurse will take you now Mrs Castle, and let's agree to meet here again at 2-00pm.'

The Consultant, Mr McGrath, pulled no punches when they met with him after lunch. 'I'm sorry to say that the news is not good. My own examination led me to think what has now been confirmed by the tests before lunch. You have carcinoma of the breast and will require immediate surgery. I shall have to completely remove your breast, what we call a radical mastectomy, which also means I shall have to remove surrounding tissues. Afterwards you will have to undergo a course of treatment of radiotherapy and cytotoxic drugs. Sometimes these can cause unpleasant side effects, but I'll get the oncologist to come and talk to you about it'.

'When are we talking about?' asked Helen,

quietly.

'Because we have a bed in the private wing empty and available, I'd like to admit you this afternoon and operate tomorrow morning.'

Billy looked at Helen, her face, as always reminding him of Anita, and knew she would face this head on, though he was less sure about Gerald who was ashen-faced.

Helen turned to Billy. 'Can you pop home and collect some night things for me? You'll find them in the middle drawer of the dressing table in our room, and things I shall need from the bathroom.'

'Of course, mum,' he replied.

'There's actually no rush,' said the nurse. 'The wing has everything you could possibly need.'

'All the same, mum will feel better with her own things. I'll go and get them when you go to the ward. By the time I get back, you'll have settled in. Dad can stay here with you.'

Helen stood and came over and kissed Gerald and Billy, and then followed the nurse out of the door to the ward.

Once they had gone, Mr McGrath began speaking again. 'I think it's only fair to warn you that I'm not entirely optimistic. Though we won't know until we have removed the tumour and tested it, the signs are not good. It seems to be a fast growing tumour and inevitably we have to take seriously the possibility of secondaries, though of course we all hope that will not be the case. I would advise you not to say this to Helen, because I find that a patient's chances are greatly enhanced by keeping a positive frame of mind. You have, I know, already been through an extremely difficult time with the death of your daughter, and some believe the development of a cancer very often follows the sort of trauma you went through then. You will need to summon up your courage to give Helen all the support she needs.'

Before he set off for home to collect Helen's necessities, Billy led Gerald to the canteen again and they sat together, each brooding on what they had just heard.

'This is more terrible than I could ever have thought possible,' said Gerald. 'First to lose Anita, and now this. I ask myself whether it isn't all pointless. I've built up a big business, a very successful business, and I'm a wealthy man — but it's worth nothing at all. It couldn't save Anita, and now Helen.'

'That's not totally true, dad. Because you can afford private care she's been seen within 24 hours by a consultant, and within a further 24 hours she will be operated on. Indirectly you've been able to do a lot. And she's not dead yet. Mum is remarkably strong.'

'Well she's always been stronger than me — I knew that from the beginning, and perhaps this illness really is what the doctor said, a sort of delayed shock. Oh, but how I wish it was me and not her. I know it sounds terrible, Billy, but I'm absolutely dreading having to face her in the ward, even before she has a operation, let alone after it.'

'I really understand that, dad, so what about we agree that you come with me now back home and help me get things together for her, and then we can come back together to be with her?'

'You're an amazing lad, Billy, son, and I wish more than anything that you had been able to marry my daughter, but I think I've got to face this and be with her today as best I can.'

Billy led Gerald, who he thought had aged decades that afternoon, to the private wing and left him at the door to make his own way in. He turned back and went to the car park and was aware that his hands were shaking as he tried to put the key into the door lock. 'Oh Anita, I need you,' he said aloud as he prepared to drive home.

Before entering the house he walked up the lane to the vicarage and was hugely relieved to discover that Hugh was in. He quickly brought him up-to-date with all that had happened in the past 24 hours. He knew he would get no platitudes but Hugh held his hand as they sat together in his study. Hugh's most religious utterance was to say, 'This is totally shitty!' When with a smile Billy asked him which bit of the Bible that came from, Hugh said, 'Believe it or not, a considerable amount of the Old Testament says that regularly, even if it tends to get a little bit lost in translation!'

'Well it seems pretty accurate to me —

perhaps I should read it.'

'Bits of it possibly,' responded Hugh. 'I'll be wholly guided by you with regard to going in and seeing her. The sudden arrival of the vicar can be a little unnerving, though the sudden arrival of the undertaker tends to be more so.'

They shook hands and Billy went to the house to do what he had come to do. At one time he knew he would have been very embarrassed having to gather nightwear and underwear from the private drawer of a lady, but this time it was possible and easy because he knew Helen was his mum, and he felt unbelievably privileged that she had asked him.

In the next few days Billy did no work, trying to spend as much time as he could with his mum. She had been told that the operation had gone well and that they were waiting for results.

'I must say, mum, considering what you've been through you look remarkable.'

'I didn't feel so good on day one but I think that was the effect of the anaesthetic, but the staff couldn't have been better. I've even been eating properly or at least as much as hospital food allows you to eat properly.'

'I imagine dad pops in straight from work.'

'He doesn't like hospitals and I don't know whether you knew, but when Anita was in here, he never came to see her – he just couldn't face it. So I'm not expecting many visits if any.'

'And have they said anything about how

long you will be here?'

'Eight to ten days, but I'm going to have to come back every single day for treatment so you might have to get used to being a taxi driver for a while rather than a curtain salesman!'

Weal and Woe

Eight days after her surgery, Helen was told she could go home on the following morning. Billy was determined to clean the house, go to the supermarket and get everything ready for her. He relaxed with a cup of tea in the middle of the afternoon, knowing that cleaning and shopping were going to be very much his daily routine in the weeks to come. The telephone rang.

'Hello Billy. It's Oliver Washington here.' Oliver was the Company Secretary who had worked with Gerald for years and was his second-in-command. 'I think you should come into the office straightaway.' He said no more and Billy needed to hear no more to be propelled to his car and set off. When he arrived he found two police cars in the car park and a police dog van parked outside on the road. Clearly something was amiss.

The first thing he noticed as he went through the front doors was the sight of police officers interviewing everyone and he assumed there must have been a robbery of some sort though he knew there was very little cash on the premises except on payday, which was not today. He went straight through to Oliver's office. 'What on earth is going on?

Oliver was direct. 'Gerald's disappeared,'

'That's ridiculous. Perhaps he's gone to the hospital to see Helen and not told anyone.'

'His car is still in the car park. He was already here when I arrived this morning. Normally I'm first in and open the place up, but he was already in his office working on papers from the safe. I thought he was in something of a state, he seemed to be shaking and not himself at all. I thought it best to let him get on with it and I went on with my own morning work. He wouldn't let anyone in, not even me, and he didn't come out for coffee with the others. Then, shortly before eleven I heard his door open and caught a glimpse of him walking down the corridor. I assumed he was going to the loo and that was the last I saw of him. A couple of the telephonists saw him going out the front door but he's not been seen since and now were talking about almost 5 hours.'

'What are the police doing?'

'In addition to questioning everyone here, apparently they're checking far and wide – the first thing they said was that he would probably be back very soon with a simple explanation, but as time passed they have become increasingly concerned.'

Billy telephoned Helen's ward to see if Gerald was there or had been in to see Helen, but the answer was no, and he asked that nothing be said to Helen about his call until he had the chance to come later.

It was not until 5:30 that the police found Gerald. Their attention had been drawn to a rope attached to a fence and leading into the river. Gerald was at the other end of the rope, having weighted his pockets with stones. It was typical of him, thought Billy, that he had made it easy for those engaged in a search to find him.

Those still at the office were devastated by the news. The police asked Billy if he would come the following morning to the Infirmary to make an official identification. What an irony. Tomorrow morning he had to be there to collect Gerald's wife. Now, however, he had to go there to tell her that her husband's dead body would rest there tonight in the mortuary.

Visiting hours were not rigorously observed in the private wing, so Billy was able to go straight in to Helen who was reading.

'I wasn't sure that I should expect you this evening, Billy. I wouldn't have minded if you hadn't come as you have to come and get me in the morning and take me home.'

'The thing is mum,' he hesitated, 'something awful has happened.'

There was a pause.

'It's Gerald isn't it?'

Billy dumbly nodded his head.

'Tell me.'

'He was in work very early and seen by Oliver working on papers from the safe, but having no contact with anyone whatsoever. Late morning he went out leaving his car in the car park and no one saw him again. They called me mid-afternoon by which time the police were searching the area and interviewing everyone. Someone out walking their dog saw a rope tied to a post going into the river and when the police came they found Gerald at the end of it with stones in his pocket.'

'Like Virginia Woolf,' said Helen. 'Oh Gerald! I feared this would happen. He was not a strong man, in fact he was so very weak in most ways. I dreaded it happening after Anita died, but this would have been just too much for him.'

'Anita would have been devastated – but I am too. I loved him,' said Billy.

'And he loved you too. He never forgave himself for what happened when Anita died, and he longed to find a way of making it up to you.'

'Even though I told him often enough that it was nothing to me now.'

'He knew he had your acceptance and total

forgiveness, but he was always appalled by what he had done, and couldn't forgive himself. Billy, I want to ask you to do me a huge favour. Because I know I'm not up to it, I'd like you to take total responsibility for the organisation of the funeral, even arranging for the food afterwards, which I think had better be in the village hall rather than at our house. I think there are bound to be a lot of people attending and we may need a sound system setting up for those outside the church who can't get in. The undertakers will arrange all that. The rest I need to leave to you.'

'I wondered what you thought about having Oliver Washington do the address. Dad thought very highly of him and they had worked together a long time.'

'I think that's an excellent idea. Over to you.'

'Mum, the police have asked me to come in here tomorrow morning to do an official identification. I really don't think you're up to doing that so soon after surgery, but if there's someone else, another member of the family say, whom you would prefer to do it, I shan't mind.'

'I'm sorry you're having to do that, but I can't think of anyone I would prefer. And you might liaise with your friend Hugh, and ask him to call in for a cup of tea in a day or two's time. Not everybody likes him in the parish, but I think he's particularly good – Anita certainly did though she was no more religious than you – and I suspect that you and he are good friends.'

'We're an unlikely combination but I think we're very close. Each of us can talk to the other about simply anything. I'm not a religious believer, as you know, though I have huge respect for what the church can do in the community in times of crisis, but I can honestly say that if I thought it would strengthen Hugh's position here, I would start going to church every Sunday. I would probably hate it but I'd be willing to do it for him.'

Billy stayed for some hours, allowing Helen to reminisce and cry about Gerald, and sharing tears with Billy about Anita. It was gone 9 o'clock when he left. He had found time to talk to the staff on the ward about what had happened and they were very attentive to Helen. Now what he needed was for circumstance to defeat the pessimism of her Consultant.

Though it was late, on arrival home the first thing he did was to visit the churchyard. He had to talk through with Anita all that happened and to give expression to his fears about Helen and what he would do if anything happened to her. It was completely dark and that was how he felt himself to be, in the dark. Yet he felt Anita saying to him, 'You can do it, my darling.'

From home he rang the undertaker, and then Hugh, who was aghast at the news which had not as yet reached him. He offered to come at once, but Billy put him off in the light of what he had to do on the following morning, but said he'd do his best to call on him later tomorrow afternoon.

'Is this Gerald Castle?' asked the policeman.

Billy looked down at the face before him, nodded his head and said 'It is.'

He had seen a lot of dead bodies, but this was the first human dead body he'd seen. The policeman and the doctor with him were kind and understanding.

'It's not an easy thing to have to do,' said the officer, 'so thank you very much indeed for coming Mr Castle, and of course your mother's here in the Infirmary as well. This must be such a difficult time for you.'

'Yes. Thank you, though I'm taking her home this morning. She had major surgery a week or so ago and she's still got to have a lot of treatment, day by day, so we'll be coming in regularly, but she really doesn't need this with her own fight to engage in.'

The doctor and police officer shook his hand and he left through the swing doors and made his way to the private wing, where Helen was ready and waiting.

'How was it?' she said.

'I suppose you could call it straightforward, like on television, but the good thing is, dad looked very peaceful and no longer agonised.'

'Thank you Billy for doing that. It's a service that a son can do for a father, and son is what you are.'

At home, Billy got his mum settled and made some lunch, and regularly received flowers at the door, many from different parts of the country, whose names were unknown even to Helen. Billy was concerned to make sure she got plenty of rest and he allowed no one to come in to see her. There were also heaps of telephone calls which he filtered, allowing only the closest of friends and family to speak to her. The undertaker wasn't due until the following day and Billy needed to have total clarity before they met as to what was required at the funeral. It was the same man who had done Anita's funeral and Billy felt odd about that, but knew that he had done a good job then and would almost certainly do so again. Late in the afternoon, having made dire threats to his mum about not answering the phone or the door, he went out having two calls to make.

The first, of course, was to Anita, and he unloaded to her the feelings, positive and negative, that had characterised his day. He stayed ages with her, but then moved out of the churchyard to the adjacent vicarage to see Hugh, who felt that he needed something stronger than the customary coffee, and quickly appeared with a gin and tonic for each of them.

'Let's deal with the living first. How's Helen?'

'She's extremely tired of course and she's soon got to begin daily radiotherapy, as well as her course of cytotoxic drugs. They've told her that she will almost certainly lose her hair – albeit temporarily, and we've been joking about what sort of wig she should get. The consultant told Gerald and me that he wasn't wildly optimistic, and that makes me really cross, because it may well be that his words contributed a great deal to what Gerald did. I'm going to try and insist that this is brought out at the inquest. I think it was totally irresponsible of him, if not worse.'

'You're not kidding. That was a terrible thing to do, especially to someone who has so recently had a major loss.'

'There's not much tonic in this, Hugh,' said Billy taking a sip.

'Shut up and drink it,' came the reply with a warm grin.

'Helen's not up to arranging the funeral so she's asked me to do that. I think she'd like to see you though, so please call when you can. I think we'd like more or less the same funeral service as we had for Anita. The only hymns I know were the ones we used to sing at school and somehow or other, from what I can remember, they wouldn't be altogether appropriate, so can we have the same ones as last time, assuming that is, you have a record of what they were.'

'I do. I always keep a record.'

'The only thing I thought that might be different would be the reading, and I wondered if you could find in the Old Testament one of those passages you mentioned to me before which express painful feelings?'

'They're called Laments, expressions of grief and loss. I can certainly look out a few for you and bring them when I come tomorrow and see what you think.'

'Thank you, I'd like that. I'm inviting a man called Oliver Washington to deliver the tribute, if that's okay with you. He worked with Gerald for a long time and probably knew the public man better than anyone else. It will be a big funeral I imagine, attended by businessmen and women from all over, including, I suspect, a contingent coming from Darlington by coach. I very much hope you will say something as well.'

'Tell the funeral director everything you want and need, and he'll deal with it — that's what he's there for and I can promise you he won't let you down, and I'll do everything I possibly can to not let you down either.'

Billy remembered from Anita's funeral that the undertaker was a jolly man. Perhaps he had to be to do his job. Though he would never have imagined it possible, Billy was aware that he succeeded in making both his mum and himself laugh. Billy, rather than Helen, did most of the talking, and the undertaker must have realised that Billy had already thought things through. He made a lot of notes and said he would liaise with the vicar on the best time for the funeral. Gerald would be buried in the grave adjacent to Anita's.

Later in the day Hugh called and Billy left him alone with Helen. He could hear tears but thought that this was something positive.

Treatment was due to begin on the following day and Billy took his mum into the radiotherapy department at the infirmary. Fortunately she didn't have to wait long, and they were soon on their way home, a journey they would have to make many times. Billy had had a long chat with Oliver on the phone who was very touched to be asked to do the tribute, and he was later due to meet with the lady in charge of the village hall to make the arrangements for the after-funeral tea. He had already alerted and booked a firm of caterers to take responsibility for it all.

'It's raining again, mum,' said Billy, shortly before they were due to leave for the church.

'I'm afraid a lot of people are going to get wet, having to stand outside the church,' she replied, 'and then we'll all get wet at the graveside.'

'Do you not think it would be better for you to leave that part of things to me? The last thing we want is you getting a cold and for the Infirmary to stop your treatment for a while.'

She sighed. 'I hadn't thought of that but you may be right. Perhaps I'll just wait in the car for you and then we can go down to the hall together.'

'Let's play it by ear. It might have stopped

raining by then, but if it hasn't I'm going to insist you go straight to the car.'

'Do you know, Billy? You sounded just like Anita then. She could be quite bossy when she knew she was right.'

'Don't I know it!'

Both Oliver and Hugh performed well and the reading he had hoped for expressed Billy's feelings admirably. The rain had not stopped and Helen was taken to the car whilst others gathered around the grave. Billy was the first to throw soil upon the coffin after it had been lowered and was aware of the puzzled looks on the faces of Gerald's brothers and sisters, as to why it should have been him doing so and not one of them. Afterwards everyone retreated to the village hall and Billy was able to greet those from the company that he had come to know, especially the ladies from Darlington, who were his favourites.

After the tea, as people were departing, Billy rescued his mum from the many people who wanted to speak to her, and took her home for a much-needed rest. Like himself, she had eaten nothing and was quite hungry and Billy said he had to go out but would be back soon and would cook for them both then. Helen knew where he was going.

Gerald's grave had already been filled in but it was to Anita's that he went.

'Thank you for standing beside me all day. I just know I couldn't have got through it without you there. My love for you has not diminished one whit. I still feel so close to you, but I want you to know that I will continue to care for and protect mum, and I promise I won't let you down in this.'

Billy suspected that those who knew he came to the churchyard each day probably thought it morbid, but it was the way he held together, regardless of what others might say or think. Hugh saw him most often, and he now knew him well as a close friend, but never had he intimated that in any way going there, to Anita, each day, was inappropriate.

After supper, in the quiet of the evening, Billy encouraged his mum to talk about Gerald.

'You might find it hard to believe but Gerald had a very ordinary upbringing, and he started his business life selling curtains on the market. He was successful because he had the gift of the gab, he really could sell snow to the Eskimos. So it wasn't long before that market stall became a business. I don't think he made many enemies, which is quite rare in business and he was certainly very shrewd in the appointments he made and decisions he took.

'We met at a social evening run by the mayor. We sort of bumped into each other and agreed that what we were at was ghastly, so we left and he took me for a meal, and the rest, as they say, is history. I had a number of miscarriages and we thought for a while that we would not have children, until Anita appeared and brought us such joy. Gerald never said he was disappointed not to have a boy who might inherit the business but I think he might have been.

'I knew early on though, that for all his success in building the business, underneath he was not at all confident in himself, that things easily threw him into a real panic, even though mostly he did his best for it not to show. I think I've said to you before that I really feared Gerald's response to losing Anita would have been his suicide, and when you came onto the ward to see me and tell me, I knew it from your face, I knew what had happened.

'Perhaps I'll never be able to tell you just how much your coming into our life has meant to us. Having lost Anita, and of course nothing could replace her, we found a son whom we have come to love so much. You were the son Gerald never had and he couldn't believe his good luck that we had found you.'

Each day they drove into the Infirmary. When Helen was receiving what apparently was increasingly known as chemotherapy, a name imported from America, it all took a long time and Billy was able to get a lot of reading done. When it was radiotherapy alone, they were often in and out in a very short while. It was however beginning to exact a heavy toll upon Helen. Once her hair began to fall out she went to see her hairdresser and had it all shaved off rather than have it come out in handfuls every day. Billy greatly admired the wigs she chose and offered to wear one himself in solidarity!

Helen had arranged with her solicitor that he should come to the house to deal with the matter of the will rather than them going to see him in town. Once he was settled with Helen, Billy made to depart.

'I rather think, Mr Castle, that it would be a good idea if you stayed here with your mother,' said the solicitor and Helen nodded her head.

He read the prologue, as Billy thought of it, and only then came to the details. These provided total security and housing for Helen for the rest of her life. Billy had not expected anything other but he still sighed with relief.

'There are various bequests to charitable foundations (he listed them), but one of some note, the sum of £10,000 to a body called The League Against Cruel Sports, "in the hope that this will please my son Billy".

'It certainly does. Thank you, Gerald. No wonder you wanted me to stay with you.'

'Yes, though I think you should stay a little longer. I come now to the company in which Gerald was majority shareholder, chairman and managing director. It is not possible to estimate what this is worth but of course it is considerable. The totality is bequeathed to you, Billy. You are now Castle's Curtains. It's your company.'

'But that's ridiculous. It should be Helen's.'

'No,' interrupted Helen. 'I was with him when he made this will, and we agreed on this together. Congratulations, my dear son.'

The New Boss

For many years afterwards Billy found himself thinking that if only Gerald had known that Helen would make a full recovery – no secondaries, no awful after-effects of the treatment – everything might have been very different. As it was, on the following morning Billy was driving Helen into the Infirmary for her regular treatment. They had spoken little since the departure of the solicitor of the news he had come to impart. Billy had been slow to take it in and Helen had not wished to push him. Now, however, she was ready to speak.

'You're going to have to impose yourself, you know. I have total confidence in you and Gerald did, but there will be opposition. Did you ever hear Gerald talking about a man called Daniel Kennedy? Perhaps you've even come across him at the office. He was undoubtedly the very worst appointment Gerald ever made. He's one of your directors and, I suppose, was brought in because he's well-connected in the business world. Actually he's a pain, and was a real thorn in Gerald's side. You're going to have to take him on and it won't be easy. Nobody will know for a few days about the new situation, but when he finds out, expect difficulties. What was that hilarious thing you told me the other day about that football manager Brian Clough assaulting one of his team's supporters?'

Billy laughed. 'I said it was the first televised occasion of a shit hitting the fan!'

'Yes that's it. Excellent. Well, when Kennedy finds out who is now in charge, it may be just like that.'

Reflecting on these words while his mum had her treatment was not encouraging to Billy. He knew he was totally unequipped in every way to do what was now asked of him. He'd said all this to Anita the previous evening, but was greeted only with silence, nor did Gerald alongside her have any wisdom to impart. Perhaps the company accountant, Matthew Taylor, who was due to come and see him later in the day, would provide him with an insight into what he should do next.

Billy had met Matthew on a number of occasions at the office and he had always been friendly, so it was a pleasure to see him when he called. With Billy's permission, their solicitor had arranged a special meeting with Matthew to let him know the circumstances in which the company now found itself. A lot of what he said went completely over Billy's head and he had to ask him to repeat himself a number of times and spell things out without the jargon most people in business take for granted. The bottom line was that the business was in very good shape though, of course, needed continual review and strong leadership.

'Will you be wanting to appoint a managing director from outside, or will you take it on yourself?'

'In the first place, until I know what is actually involved, I don't think it would be right for me to try and appoint someone else to do the job. In any case it would take some time to advertise and interview before an appointment could be made. No. This is what Gerald wanted and this is what Gerald will get.'

'In which case, once all this is public knowledge your first act must be to call a Board Meeting for which you will need to prepare carefully with Oliver. Forgive me asking, but have you ever chaired a meeting before?'

'No, never. I don't think I've ever attended a meeting,'

'In which case that makes it even more imperative that you spend time with Oliver, going through the process. In any case you wouldn't chair the first meeting of the Board, someone else will do that and you can learn from what happens, but you are by far and away the principal shareholder, and they will know that it's your place to be chairman next time. Now I think of it Mr Castle, there are some very good books available from the Institute of Directors and the Industrial Society which could help you a great deal as you settle in, and certainly you should look to join the Institute of Directors. You won't be the youngest. There are some very fine young entrepreneurs out there, and it may well be worth your while getting to know some of them.'

'Tell me, will I be in a position to sack Mr Kennedy?'

'I suppose you might try, but I'd give it time. You might even get on, though I suspect it's more likely that he will see your relative youth and inexperience as an opportunity to manipulate you.'

'This is slightly embarrassing question Matthew, because it concerns my own financial position. Until now I haven't had one and I imagine that has now changed.'

'Obviously I'm not your personal accountant, though I can direct you to someone I would heartily recommend, because I concentrate on businesses, but there can be no doubt, given your shareholding, that you are a very wealthy man. If you chose to sell the business, by selling your shares, your capital would be considerable –

well into the higher millions. As managing director your salary will be considerably higher than that of anyone else in the company.'

'Jesus,' uttered Billy.

'Gerald thought extremely highly of you and said you'd had a pretty grim beginning. He told me of the quality of the personnel management you had in effect been doing for him and I know, that had he survived, you might well have soon become the Personnel Director, highly paid and on the Board. Now it's up to you. He thought you can do it. Prove him right. I will do everything in my ability to support you. One final thing though. Please continue to be yourself.'

'Matthew, I can't thank you enough. You've said to me today what I wanted and needed to hear. You even make me think I can do this.'

Matthew having departed, Billy and his mum enjoyed a cup of tea and a piece of ginger cake together, and he went over all that Matthew had said. They now needed to decide when all this should be made public. The business had no PR adviser, but when Billy was on the phone to the Institute of Directors they recommended a firm who would be of real service. After speaking to them they arranged for someone from the Financial Times to come and see him, an interview at which they would themselves be present to guide him. There was something in Billy that thought that all this was funny, that it had the quality of dream verging on nightmare. He went to see Anita that evening, and ever conscious of Gerald next door, told her everything that had happened. He even said that given his new station in life, the hunt would no doubt offer him tickets for the Hunt Ball, which he thought was an absolute hoot and she agreed.

A week later the story appeared in the newspaper and was quickly taken up by local television and radio. The advice of the PR adviser who came to be with him was to say very little about himself and his past, and concentrate instead on how strong the business was and ripe for further development.

On the eve of Billy's entrance into his new world, Oliver Washington came to see him and they went through all the things Billy needed to know when he arrived. He had been reading books about management and chairing meetings, but took great comfort from knowing that he would have Oliver at his side.

Having done the Infirmary trip, Billy, suitably attired in a new bespoke suit his mum approved of, set-off for his workplace. He pulled into Gerald's vacant space in the car park, hesitated before he got out, but then made his way through the front doors. There to greet him were many of the workforce and all the directors, who shook his hand and congratulated him, even Daniel Kennedy.

'It's lovely to see you all again. I've missed

you – no, really, I have. I want to thank so many of you for your presence at the funeral, for flowers and cards and other tokens of your concern. I know how much my mum and I appreciated them. We are still going through a difficult time as she recovers from surgery and has ongoing treatment each day, but I can tell you with absolute certainty, we are going to win that battle.'

'Hear hear,' said a number of voices.

'Now it's back to reality and for me the steepest of learning curves in which I shall need all of you to be patient. I have a lot to learn but this is a great business and it's going to be greater.'

Applause broke out.

'Finally can I just say how appalled I am that so many of you are here lounging about, when you should be working! But thank you.'

There was laughter and further applause as Billy made his way to what he inevitably still thought of as Gerald's office. As he was hanging his coat up behind the open office door, he heard Kennedy say to another director, 'That was very good.' Billy breathed a great sigh of relief.

A month or so later, which had been one of massive learning but had gone surprisingly well, including the first Board Meeting, Billy asked Daniel Kennedy if he would call in and see him. He was cautious in his dealings with him because of his reputation but had actually found nothing to substantiate it and he was clearly a wise businessman.

'Daniel, I'd like to appoint a personnel manager, not just for here but across the whole business. He or she would do what I was doing for Gerald and will oversee appointments and deal with issues that inevitably arise among the workforce from time to time. What do you think?'

'I think it's a great idea, Billy, and I'm pretty sure once he saw how you were doing the job, Gerald would have soon come to the same conclusion. It will be your appointment, your first appointment, so get it right!'

'Daniel, before I began this job a number of people whom I won't name, warned me about you. It was said you were awkward and difficult, and almost certainly committed murder in your spare time. The thing is I haven't found this to be the case at all. You're always warm, friendly and utterly supportive. Any thoughts?'

'I wonder how they found out about the murders! But seriously I suppose I can understand it. I did not see eye to eye with Gerald on a lot of matters. He was, and I say this knowing how close you were to him, diligent and hard-working, but I always felt he lacked imagination and couldn't really see how things could be different and better. So I guess I came over as difficult. When we received the news that you were taking over, I was at first shocked and, to be honest, appalled, and I expected that you would quickly go under. But from your first weeks here I've realised that you're very much your own man and not just a clone of Gerald, and that you're open to the sorts of changes we need to take us forward. I'm really impressed that we now have a PR firm looking after us, which you brought in, that our MD is a member of the Institute of Directors, and now you're talking about a personnel manager. What is there to complain about?'

Helen's treatment eventually came to an end, and although she was still wearing a wig, her hair was beginning to grow. Billy asked if she thought she was up to a winter break and so they flew to Vienna. They didn't do a lot – Helen really wasn't up to doing much — but they did eat a lot of disgusting chocolate torte, and drank strong coffee. They did, however, get to the Spanish Riding School to see the wonderful white horses perform.

One morning in a cafe, Helen raised what she feared was a particularly sensitive matter with Billy.

'I've noticed, Billy, and living in the same house as you I could hardly miss it, that one thing that has not been part of your life since Anita, is a girlfriend. And I just wondered whether this was because you thought I wouldn't approve?'

'I was thinking about that the other day myself. Just about the only girls I've met in the last couple of years have been curtain machinists in Darlington, and delightful though they are, none have exactly taken my fancy. The fact is, mum, I don't have much contact with girls or women of my own age.'

'I realise that and you may have to do something about it, though I don't know what that would be, but what I wanted to say more than anything was that I'd be delighted if you did have a girlfriend. After all I want to have grandchildren, and the only route to that is through you. I know, Billy, that Anita is still at the centre of your heart, but life has to go on, and for you too, and I'm absolutely certain that Anita would not want it any other way.'

After the holiday Billy made his way, as usual, up to the churchyard, and spoke about what his mum had said, adding that he didn't want to betray her, Anita, by loving another. Once again she seemed to say little to him and he began to make his way back home, but passing the vicarage the door opened and Hugh stood there, clearly not entirely at peace with the world. Billy went in.

'I can't take any more, Billy. I've tried, you know I've tried, but they've won.'

'They?'

'The county set, those who come to the church and think they own it and treat me as if I were a paid servant. They are totally opposed to everything that just might keep me here — the ideas I have of using the church building during the week as a sort of community centre, of setting up a network of carers for the old people and lonely, and of course they are totally opposed to the use of the new services. As it is, these would have just been compromises for me. I'm disaffected with it all and I have no desire to do it any more. I've told the family and rang up the bishop this afternoon and told him I wanted to sign a deed of resignation at once. He, perhaps wisely, told me to wait until we had found somewhere to live, and I don't know where that will be or how we will be able to afford to do it, or what work there might be, but I have to go, and I really don't want to take any more services in that building for those people. I shall go to the doctor and ask him to sign me off, and then it will be up to the rural Dean to provide retired clergy to take the services.'

'I think you knew that this day would come, sooner or later, Hugh, and although I'm hugely saddened by it because your care for my family has been second to none, I think that what you're doing is right. But, you know, it occurs to me that your outlook may not be quite as bleak as you imagine. I'm looking to appoint a personnel manager who would be on a salary considerably greater than the one you are on at the moment and would probably allow you to get a mortgage. Whoever is appointed will have to do a fair bit of driving around the place, visiting all our depots and agents across the country, but you'd be very much your own boss and reporting directly to me.'

'But how on earth would I stand a chance

being appointed in competition with those already doing that sort of work in business. I know nothing about it.'

'Hugh, I'm the managing director and I don't know very much about it! Besides which, who said anything about competition. If you and Veronica think this is a possibility, then you'd be the only candidate, and believe you me we won't be asking your congregation for a reference.'

'And you can do this, give someone a job just like this?'

'Hugh, I can do what I like, but I tell you what, come to the office tomorrow morning and have a look and we'll talk about salary, expenses and of course, a company car. You would really enjoy this job and be good at it. In part it's what I was doing when I was working for Gerald and I loved it.'

On the following morning Hugh accepted the position and Oliver said he would draw up a contract for each party to sign in due course. Billy showed him round and introduced him to just about everyone who worked there.

'I shall never be able to thank you enough for this, Billy,' said Hugh as he prepared to leave.

'Nonsense. If I hadn't believed you could do the job, and do it well, I wouldn't have suggested it. I'm not just doing you a favour so much as making what I hope and think is a good decision for the company. You will need to get on with looking for somewhere to live, and when you're ready to start you and I can possibly do some trips away together to visit what we call the outstations. Not only can I introduce you, but hardly anyone has seen me in my new role as MD. And there's no reason why we shouldn't have a good time while we are about it.'

One evening two weeks later, Billy had fallen asleep in front of the television and Helen was knitting, when the telephone rang. She answered it and at once woke Billy up.

'It's Matthew Taylor. He says he needs to speak with you urgently.'

Billy looked at his watch — it was almost 9:30.

'Hello Matthew. This is late for you to call.'

'I need to see you straightaway, this evening, now, it can't wait. I need to see both of you.'

'Of course. Come at once.'

Billy and Helen looked at one another. Matthew arrived 15 minutes plater, carrying a large briefcase and began speaking at once.

'Everything can be sorted if you answer yes to the question I'm going to ask: Have you withdrawn a considerable sum of money from the firm's No.3 account?'

'Of corse not and for two simple reasons. The first is that I didn't know we had such an account. I knew about 1 and 2, but as yet you have never told me that there was a 3. And second, even if I had known it existed I wouldn't have had the first idea how to withdraw anything from it. I've only been around a short while and though you've tried to teach me, my financial knowledge of the business is still rudimentary.'

'I knew of course what your answer would be, but I had to ask the question. The No.3 account about which I imagine Helen is well aware, was Gerald's own emergency account, there to meet immediate need if circumstances demanded it. We are talking about your money, Billy, what you have inherited.'

'I knew about it of course,' said Helen, 'but to be honest Matthew I'd completely forgotten all about it. Gerald opened it quite some time ago as far as I can recall but I've no idea how much is in it.'

'Well the answer is, a lot less than there should be. Until the last few days there was £150,000 give or take. Someone has now removed £60,000 in one go and to be honest it's a sheer accident that I found this out because normally I only check it once a year, but I thought that with Billy taking over I ought just to find out how much was there as I thought he needed to know.'

'Do you think someone knew that you wouldn't need to look into this account until next year at the earliest and thereby leaving the trail cold?' asked Billy.

'That's exactly what I think.'

The three of them sat in silence, each

wondering what to say next. It was Billy who asked the question, 'What do we have to do next, Matthew?'

'I'm afraid there is no alternative. We have to go to the police and to the specialist department dealing with business matters, and we have to do it first thing in the morning.'

'I agree.'

'There's a Detective Chief Inspector Bob Wakeham, whom I know through Rotary, who heads the financial unit. With your agreement I'm going to telephone him this evening. I know it's late, but I need to alert him. Until he gives the word, I think it's vital we say nothing at the office. Whoever's done this mustn't know that an investigation is being carried out, until Bob says so.'

'That's fine by me. Where shall we meet?'

'I'll pick you up at 8 o'clock from here. You may need to develop a cold overnight to explain your absence to your secretary.'

'A cold feels like the least of my worries.'

Billy found it hard to get to sleep, going over and over in his mind how this could have happened and who might have done it. He did take some comfort from the fact that he knew so little about company finances that it wasn't going to fall to him to find out who had been fiddling the books. He thought back to his days at the kennels where his biggest anxiety was over the question of whether he should skin a cow tonight or leave it until morning — something that had never kept him awake. In the half-light of dawn he looked across his room and saw his picture of Anita. He felt certain that she would want him to rise to the occasion and would have full confidence in him.

Chief Inspector Wakeham was a big man and, according to Matthew, a pretty fine rugby player in his younger days. He told Billy that he had specialised in financial matters more or less from the beginning of his time in the City of London police force. Later he and his wife moved out of London and he was heading the unit which dealt with these matters across the county.

Having gone through the books in some considerable detail with Matthew and another officer from the unit, he sought to ascertain from Billy how much understanding he had of the matters in hand, given that he had only recently taken over the company. Out of 10, Billy scored about 3, and Bob, with a smile, said that he still had a lot to learn.

'Oh I'm well aware of that.'

'At least I know from your answers that there is simply no possibility of you being a suspect. In any case it would make no sense. The money that's been stolen is your money so you're hardly likely to have stolen it from yourself, even if you knew how and it's pretty obvious you don't. Perfect alibi.'

'So where do we go from here?'

'We need from you and Matthew a list of those who would have known of the existence of this account, and who would have had the acumen to get access to it.'

'Matthew will know this better than me, but I suspect that the list is going to be short.'

Matthew silently nodded in agreement.

'And do you want your investigation to remain a secret?'

'For now. We'll do some background work on the people on the list – that may even bring us the answer we're looking for. You'd be amazed how many villains exercise extreme caution and cunning in one part of their enterprise and when they think they've got away with it behave utterly stupidly and give themselves away. That might happen in this case but we'll see. If you can give me a list of names now, before you leave, we can get on with this. We might strike gold and if we don't it will mean our big feet trampling all over your works, but let's hope it doesn't come to that.'

The list Matthew and Billy drew up was short. They surmised that it had to be someone in head office — that this was totally outside the frame of reference of anyone in the outstations or working as agents. Daniel Kennedy as finance director would almost certainly have known about the account, as would one of the other directors, Joshua Henderson, who had worked closely with

Gerald and had already indicated to Billy his intention of standing down. There was Billy's secretary, Vicky Chapman, who had been Gerald's secretary for a long time, whose name had to be added, but whom they both discounted. The only other name they could think of was Oliver Washington, and again they both discounted the possibility that he could have been involved.

A whole week went by and they heard nothing, when one late morning Bob Wakeham himself turned up at Billy's office and was shown in by Vicky.

'Getting straight to the point,' he said, 'I wanted you to know that within the last hour we have arrested and charged Oliver Washington with the theft of £60,000 from your No.3 account. He has admitted the offence and will be appearing before magistrates tomorrow. We are keeping him in custody overnight primarily for his own protection.'

'What on earth do you mean?'

'I think from the beginning we were misled by you and Matthew saying that it could not possibly be Oliver, that he had to be innocent. It turned out he wasn't quite as innocent as you thought. As I said to you on a previous occasion he used great skill to acquire the money and behaved utterly stupidly when he came to spend it. He used it to buy a house in town for a girlfriend. She was already known to us and had a number of charges against her name for soliciting — she is a tom who probably wanted to settle down and saw Oliver as her best chance. The person he needs protecting from is his wife'.

Billy sat back in his chair and turned slightly away to look out the window.

'Is he likely to go to prison?'

'Almost certainly, though by pleading guilty he'll get a shorter sentence.'

With the police officer gone, Billy first telephoned his mum who could hardly believe what she was hearing, and then Matthew, who was as shocked as he was himself. He then decided to go straight home to be with his mum, and to visit Gerald and Anita in the churchyard. He felt utterly overwhelmed by it all. It turned out, on arrival, that Helen had been already forced to the conclusion that it must be Oliver who was responsible, even though she didn't want to believe it. He was the only person who had the knowledge and the means.

'I suppose we all have our weaknesses and when temptation comes it's not always easy to resist. We know nothing about Oliver's home life and whether he was unhappy. I think he must have been desperate and I really don't want to judge him,' she said.

Sonja with a J

Though he would not have said so to anyone,
except Anita, Billy was getting bored and restless
running the business. Surely there has to be more
to life than making lots of money, he thought to
himself. He did at least have a few good days away
travelling with Hugh who had now begun work
and seemed to be enjoying his new job. They
talked a lot as they drove, and Billy realised how
much he was missing the kind of intellectual
stimulation he and Hugh had offered one another.
Running a company, even though he had to admit
he was growing into the role, clearly used a
different part of his brain.

      His former tutors at the college had told him

he was now well equipped to apply to study at university. An idea had formed in his mind about what he would like to study, if he were to do so, but the real difficulty would be to know what to do about the company. Perhaps there was a way of giving up the role of managing director and remaining chairman, and of course if all else failed, he could pull out completely and sell-up, though he didn't feel that would be right — at least not at the present time, so he had made an appointment to meet with one of his his former tutors at the college to talk it through. Bored at work, he left and drove to the college ludicrously early. Hoping that the canteen would be open he went in and found it empty apart from just one member of staff behind the counter. Billy was immediately taken with her. She was short and slim (a combination he favoured), but he was struck by her perfect face with high cheek-bones and jet black hair in a pony-tail. He ordered a cup of tea from her and she said she would bring it over. Her accent suggested Eastern Europe, perhaps Poland. He sat down and waited.

'Would you be able to sit with me a while?' he asked, when she arrived.

'Thank you. I should like that. We are between the day students and those who come in the evening, so it's usually very quiet at this time of day. What are you? Day student or night class?'

'I'm not doing a course at the moment, but I'm here to see someone about the possibility of doing so. But tell me about you. What is your name?'

'I'm Sonja with a J. I left Communist Poland three years ago with my daughter Marja, and my sister. We live together here in town. You can see the work I do, and my sister Katja, also with a J, works as a cleaner six mornings a week, though in Poland she was a fully qualified dentist.'

'And she can't get work here?'

'Her qualifications are not recognised without a further year of full-time study. So she's trying to save money, but it will take a long time.'

'And what about Marja's father - your husband perhaps?'

'I'm ashamed to say I only met him once, a regrettable evening in Kiev, a handsome sweet-talking Ukrainian soldier who talked me into his bed when I was feeling lonely, and whose name I never even knew. Not my finest hour, but I adore my Marja, and wouldn't be without her for anything.'

Billy smiled. 'And do you have a boyfriend now?'

'When would I have the time for a boyfriend?'

Billy was aware that he felt glad to hear it but not exactly sure why.

'What is your background?'

'I have a degree in mathematics and I am also qualified in business studies. As you may know, the state controls everything in Poland, though I believe it will change one day. I worked in a heavy engineering factory as a financial manager. It was okay for at least it used my skills, which is considerably more than this job does, but being foreign does not lend itself to good employment opportunities in England. Perhaps if I was to study for an MBA it might be easier, but you have to be working in a company to do that. I think it is what the Americans call a "Catch-22" situation. But I have told you all this and I do not even know your name.'

'My name is Billy Castle and I was born here in this town. I had a very unhappy childhood and left school at 16 to work in a sort of animal slaughter yard. But now, and you may find this hard to believe, given my age, but by a series of painful and unusual circumstances, I find myself the chairman and managing director of a large local company. This was something I inherited and certainly did not earn. It came to me following the death of a man I came to call my father after he and his wife took me in and sort of adopted me following the death of their daughter, my girlfriend Anita. They regarded me as their son and I still live at home with my mum, Helen. Her husband, Gerald, my adopted father, took his own life in tragic and unnecessary circumstances, and to everyone's amazement, but especially mine, I discovered that he had bequeathed to me the company. Perhaps you have heard of it, "Castle's Curtains".'

Sonja rose from her chair and went behind the counter for a moment, reappearing with another drink for Billy.

'That is quite a story.'

'I think it's even more complicated than that, but that will do for the present.'

'And are you married or have a girlfriend?'

'I suppose I would give the same answer that you did — when would I have the time? Besides which there are those whom I trust, who think I'm still too wedded to the memory of Anita because I visit her grave every day and talk to her. Perhaps they're right, but it has become such a pattern of my daily living that I wouldn't know how to change it.'

Billy looked at his watch. 'Look, Sonja with a J, I'm going to have to go or I'll be late for my appointment, but it strikes me that you and I might be able to be of great service to one another – work-wise I mean. I want to put an idea to you because I have a feeling that you might be exactly the right person we need at the office. Would you be willing to meet with me, say, tomorrow morning, and let me outline what I have in mind?'

'Marja will be at play school from 9:30 until 12. I could meet you then. Would you like to come to our flat?'

'I don't think that would be altogether appropriate until you know me better, and can trust that what I'm saying is true and not just fantasy. I don't want you to think that I'm like a sweet talking Ukrainian soldier. There is a quiet teashop, I think it's called "Daphne's Tea Rooms", in Radipole Lane, just down from the library. How would it be if we did something very English together, and you let me buy you a coffee and toasted teacake, allowing us time for me to present something to you which you might find could make a significant difference to your life here?'

'I would like that very much, Mr Castle.'

'I'm afraid it won't happen at all unless you call me Billy!'

She reached across and touched his hand. 'Billy.'

He reached into his pocket and produced a business card on which he scribbled a number. 'That's my home number. If you change your mind or if there's a problem, call me at home tonight or at work in the morning. But I hope there will be no problems and I'm already looking forward to morning.'

They both smiled.

When Billy arrived for his appointment there was just one thing on his mind — Sonja, and he could barely get her out of it. Billy briefly told his former tutor how the circumstances of his life had radically changed and that he was now a major businessman in the area, but that he was easily bored by it though endlessly busy, and increasingly felt that he needed intellectual stretching, and not merely the grind of accounts and planning and all the sorts of things he had to do day by day.

'Do you think,' he asked, 'I should explore once again the possibility of doing a university course?'

'An undergraduate degree course is a full-time activity and usually takes three years. Even if you did it nearby, at Reading say, and were based at home, I don't see how you could possibly fit it in to what is obviously an extremely busy life. I just don't think it would be sustainable to do a degree, whilst trying to run a business as you do, without being able to absent yourself for the best part of three years from your work and your responsibilities to others.'

'And there's no way, at least at present, that I could possibly do that.'

As he drove home, Billy felt a strange mixture of deflation and burgeoning joy. He had probably known all along that the possibility of a degree was not great and had now had that confirmed, but there was something else he was aware of that made him feel good and it was called Sonja with a J.

Although he made his daily visit to Anita, it was shorter than usual, and only on his way back did he remember that he had forgotten to tell her about Sonja. At this stage too, he said nothing to his mum, besides which, what was there to say? All that had happened was that he believed he had solved the problem of replacing Oliver, which reminded him that he was due on the following afternoon to visit Mrs Washington at their home. Oliver had been granted bail by the magistrates, though committed for trial, but apparently his wife refused to let him come home and had had all the locks changed.

Billy had not been in the tea rooms for a while, but was pleased to see they were unchanged. He thought all waitresses ought to wear black dresses, frilly aprons and hats, though where in his bizarre upbringing he had ever acquired such a fantasy, he couldn't think.

He chose a table and within just a few seconds saw Sonja enter. She removed her coat and sat down with an uncertain look on her face. Billy felt it would not be entirely the right thing for him to comment on her appearance, but he could not deny to himself that she looked so very lovely.

'I will come to the point immediately so you are not left wondering what is to come.'

'I would appreciate that.'

'I would like to appoint you as our Company Secretary. I don't know whether in the context of the Polish political situation you had such things, but here it is a senior position. You will be a member of the Board and in effect responsible for running the company on a day-to-day basis, with particular reference to financial matters. It will be well paid with a company pension and the provision of a company car. You may meet a measure of opposition, but somehow I think you will be able to handle that relatively easily, and when they see that you are doing a good job, which I have no doubt you will do, you will easily win them over. At all times you will have my total support and backing.'

Coffee and teacakes arrived which Billy at once began to devour, leaving Sonja quite dumb.

'Why would you do this for me?' she eventually said.

'Once upon a time, as I told you last night, I found myself doing the most awful job you could ever imagine. I was rescued from that and given opportunities beyond my imagination. When I met you yesterday — gosh, was it only yesterday? — I was instantly drawn to you, you might call it intuition, and when you told me your story I immediately thought that my pressing need to get a Company Secretary could be met by your pressing need to stop being a server of tea and to become instead what you're meant to be. I saw me in you and a chance to do for someone else what had been done for me.'

He persuaded her to have a drink and some teacake which she did. He could see she was shaking and he wanted to take hold of her hand but thought it best not to do so.

'I have brought you some papers which outline the present situation of the company, and if you take the job, which I hope you will, I would like you to do a sort of induction with my good friend Hugh, who is the newly appointed personnel manager. He will take you round what we call the outstations of the business so you can see how we function. You'll like him. He's my closest friend and a very wise person. If you're interested in the job, I'd like to meet you at the office and show you round. We don't actually make curtains here, they are made up in the North of England in a place called Darlington which you will greatly enjoy visiting. If you will accept my offer, the details of which we can handle when you come to the office. The only other question is when can you start?

'I do not need to think about it, Billy. I accept your offer and I can start whenever you want me to, tomorrow if need be, though I will need to make arrangements for Marja's care in the mornings but I'm sure that can be quickly sorted. What about a contract?'

Billy laughed. 'As Company Secretary, your first task will be to draw up your own contract. It will have be agreed by the Board of course, but it should be plain sailing.'

Before they left, Sonja shook hands with Billy to seal her appointment. Billy had to suppress a strong desire to kiss her.

Even as he drove to see Mrs Washington, an interview to which he was not looking forward, it was Sonja who occupied his thoughts. Life was certainly unpredictable. Who could possibly have thought that, of all people, Oliver would have taken a former prostitute as his mistress, and stolen

£60,000 to provide her with a house? Yet had it not taken place in this way, he would never have been able to offer work to Sonja.

It was a smart modern house on a small estate and Billy found it easily because of the firm's car parked outside on the drive. Madeline Washington was in her late-40s, rather plain, and from what Helen had told him worked as a pharmacist. Billy's first thought was that she looked exhausted, as indeed she must be. She let him in and offered a cup of coffee which he accepted.

'Oliver was devastated by Gerald's death for they had worked so closely together for such a long time, and he was pretty thrown by your appointment, if you don't mind me saying so. He felt it was totally ridiculous, but none of this had anything to do whatsoever with what he did. I don't know whether you know, probably you do, that Marilyn — that's her name – was, is, a prostitute in Reading. She didn't appear in the magistrates court though I gather from the police that she has done on a number of previous occasions on charges of soliciting. The police told me that she is past her best — years of drugs, cigarettes and all that is involved in working the streets as a tom, as they call it. God only knows what he saw in her — well sex obviously – but according to the police she says he became very possessive, wanting to keep her for himself and paying more and more in the hope that she would abandon the game. Then he offered her a house and said he would pay for it, just like that. Do you know, one of the police officers said to me confidentially, "To be honest Mrs Washington, I cannot possibly see what he sees in her, she's an old slag and junkie"?'

Billy said nothing.

'I remember some time ago Oliver saying to me that he thought there was no meaning in life at all, that it was all a joke, and all we could do was live for today. He was very deeply affected when your Anita died. He didn't know her particularly well but it was just the fact of it, the pointlessness. It hit him very hard. Perhaps that's why he went off the rails. To be fair to him I had pretty much gone off sex and it was clearly totally different for him. But why turn to her? I just can't fathom it out.'

Billy felt totally out of his depth and wished he could have had Hugh there with him. He would have known how to handle the situation, and what to say and not say. But Hugh was not there – he was.

'There are some practicalities I need to deal with. Holiday pay, in the main, to which Oliver is due, and I'm afraid the company car will have to be returned. When the new Company Secretary is in place, proper arrangements will be made with regard to Oliver's pension. If you are in touch with him at all, then I would be grateful if you could inform him of this. As you may know he is not allowed to come to the office – it's one of the conditions of his bail, and we have no way of contacting him.'

'So you've replaced him already?'

'Just about. Companies have to keep functioning.'

'And what about the money he stole? Will you get that back? I gather from the police that it's your personal money.'

'Personal money that I knew nothing about but, yes, the house Oliver bought will be sold and the proceeds returned.'

'If I may ask how are you getting on doing the job you must have felt totally unprepared for?'

'I suppose I have found that the best way of handling it all is to take advice and then make my own mind up. But I'm not meant to be a businessman, that much I do know, so I have no idea whatsoever what the future holds except that in the meantime I will continue to do my very best for the company and in memory of Gerald who must've had too much to drink on the day he signed his will and left it all to me.'

'And how is Helen?'

'As far as we can tell, and as far as the doctors know, she has made a full recovery from her cancer and she keeps busy in the village and looking after me. I think she would like me to find a nice girl and settle down but the truth is I don't come across many young women to whom I take a fancy. However, I'm still very young and I've got years ahead of me.'

Mrs Washington smiled at him. 'You sound very wise to me, Billy. My only advice is to keep away from the prostitutes of Reading!'

'Do you know, I rather thought I would.'

Sonja telephoned to arrange her visit to the office.

'I've managed to get proper childcare for Marja. Katja has contacts at the Polish Church, and she's been accepted for their playgroup.'

' I suppose most Poles are Catholics.'

'It was the one organisation that enabled us to stand up to the communists. We were all baptised and huge numbers go to church. With a Polish pope now in place the churches are even stronger and the communist state is on the back foot. It will fall. But that doesn't imply we are all believers. I am not, though my sister goes to Mass every Sunday. For her, I think it is a way of keeping in touch with other people from Poland rather than a particularly religious thing, but maybe I'm wrong.'

'I'm not a believer either.' replied Billy, 'I couldn't be.'

'Because of Anita?

'Amongst other things, yes. There's so much to tell you,' he said mysteriously, and wondered just what he was saying and meaning by it.

Before her arrival at the office, Billy sent a memo to everyone about her appointment. He had already spoken informally to the directors one by one and told them. Daniel the difficult, as he was sometimes known, though never to Billy who liked him enormously and worked well with him, a good source of sound advice, roared with laughter, and said that if she turned out to be as good as Hugh, it would be a great appointment. The memo left everyone else intrigued.

'I expect the college was disappointed to lose you as their tea lady,' said Billy to Sonja jokingly.

'I don't care. I didn't go back. I telephoned and said I was leaving. They did not seem particularly concerned. I had never been given a contract and they very often rang me at short notice and said I wasn't required. It's not untypical for casual labour, especially if you're a foreigner.'

'You won't be a casual labourer here, I can assure you, and already people are very much looking forward to meeting you. I have not had a single adverse comment. I'll show you round and you can meet the staff before we get together with Hugh, your personnel manager.'

Billy thought she looked simply adorable, and as they walked round together meeting everyone he could tell she made quite an impression. He then led her to the Boardroom where Daniel and Hugh at once stood up and welcomed her, Daniel noticeably looking her up and down. They chatted for a while over coffee, mostly business talk which was foreign to Billy and, probably, Hugh, though he made a great effort to take part. Oliver's car had been cleaned and made ready for her on its return from Mrs Washington and they would date her commencement of work from today.

'I must congratulate you, Billy, on your appointment,' said Daniel, 'you have chosen well. You, Miss Kosko, clearly have a good understanding of the way businesses work. Every one is different, of course, but I hope that within a short time you will feel completely on top of what we are doing.'

'Thank you, but please, you must call me Sonja. "Miss Kosko" sounds like an old lady.'

'I don't think anybody is likely to make that mistake,' said Daniel.

Billy took a blushing Sonja with him to his office.

'Hugh will be joining us shortly to discuss with you the possibilities of going with him to see the rest of the company at work throughout the country. I used to do that and I really enjoyed it, but there is work here that already needs your attention and I very much hope that from tomorrow you will get on with it. Your predecessor, Oliver Washington, worked with my dad Gerald for a long time but for reasons I just don't understand, and his wife doesn't understand, he got into a liaison with a prostitute, as a result of which he stole £60,000 from one of our accounts to set her up in a house. He has been sent to trial and the police tell me he will probably be going to prison. It's so sad really, and his wife is devastated. But what it means is that no one has been doing his work for quite some time and we need you first and foremost to do a rescue act. We will be getting that money back. Technically it's my personal money, not the company's, but that is of no importance. We need you to get us back on our feet and I suggest that, if you are able, you spend the rest of the day with your secretary Ellie Dowson, working out your priorities before you get going on them. Ellie was very much affected by what Oliver has done. She is very good indeed but please do your best to look after her. One other thing, Sonja, although I am your boss, please do your best to look after me too.'

Billy's mum, Helen, was amused and impressed by his new appointment, as he spoke about her at length each evening when he arrived home. By now he had also begun talking about her to Anita on his daily visit to the churchyard, and he felt her pleasure.

'I've told you before, Billy, that if ever you entered into a relationship I would be nothing but happy for you. You and I are very close, made closer by our shared deaths of Anita and Gerald, and I believe that nothing will separate us. I am your mum and you are my son. You are a very eligible and good-looking young man. Someone will come along who will be the right person for you at this time in your life. Anita was then, and God only knows I would give everything to have her back as I'm sure you would, and no one will ever replace her, but someone will be wholly new and bring you great joy, and bring me grandchildren.'

'You are the most wonderful mum in the world. I love you very much and would never do anything to hurt you under any circumstances. I know what you're saying is true and that it's probably unhealthy of me to go to Anita each day but I will stop when she tells me to stop.'

'I know. And strangely, it comforts me to see you walking up the lane each evening, though I suspect you miss Hugh's presence there.'

'I see him at work of course, though we rarely have the time to talk as we used to. I must do something about that, build into our schedules times when we can perhaps pop out in the middle of the day and go to a pub for a drink. I'm not sure slave driver Sonja will approve, but I'm boss, not her.'

'Are you sure she knows that?'

Trial Without Jury

Billy's first appearance in court that month was for Gerald's inquest. He was impressed by the coroner and her concern to make this as painless as possible. When he was asked to give evidence, however, he felt it totally incumbent upon him to refer to the way in which the consultant at the Infirmary had spoken to Gerald and himself and given them a bleak picture. He was sure that this conversation had played a major part in Gerald's decision to commit suicide. The coroner said she noted what he said and would make recommendations to the Infirmary with regard to speculation about prognosis to relatives. Billy had hoped for more, possibly a note of censure sent to the surgeon involved, but Helen said that such a response from the coroner would not bring Gerald back, and Billy reluctantly decided to let his strong feelings go.

A couple of weeks later, Helen told Billy that she wanted to meet his new Company Secretary, and he instructed him to invite her for supper. He did his mother's bidding and Sonja accepted the invitation immediately. They came in two cars straight from work and after introducing Sonja to Helen, Billy offered to provide Sonja with a guided tour of the village before it got dark, and as they set out Billy noticed Helen watching from the kitchen window and was sure she was smiling as he began the grand tour with the churchyard.

They stood before Anita's and Gerald's graves.

'Your name is on the stone: "Beloved of Billy". That is so good.'

'The first thing I knew of it was when it appeared. It was a great surprise.'

'Your mother is a good woman, I think.'

'Not least when you consider that her teenage daughter died, her husband committed suicide and she has had cancer.'

'Do you feel you have to run the business for her sake?'

'I'm not sure I know how to answer that question. She has told me that I'm totally free to leave it, to sell the business if I feel I can't go on with it, but it's the family business and I feel under some sort of obligation.'

'You have said to me that you are sometimes very bored by what you have to do each day, and aren't you wanting to do more study? If you remember, that is how we met when you came to the college to discuss it.'

'I haven't forgotten how we met, believe you me. Now we must go home and get some of mum's cooking.'

When he reflected upon it later, a strange thing happened as they began to walk down the lane. Quite unaware of it, he found himself holding hands with Sonja, as if for each it was the most natural thing in the world and that they had not needed to give any thought to it.

'I've taken a great risk Sonja, and made for us Bigos, and if you don't eat meat I'm in real trouble,' said Helen, as she brought to the table a rich smelling Polish stew.

'Oh thank you Mrs Castle, that is so thoughtful of you.'

'I shall take it away again if you don't call me Helen.'

'Please don't do that. . . Helen.'

'So where is Marja this evening?' asked Helen.

'My sister Katja is looking after her.'

'It was very remiss of Billy not to include them in the invitation to come this evening. I would very much like to meet them.'

'Thank you. Marja starts school soon and of course she speaks English perfectly, not with the accent her mother has.'

'I think your English is simply brilliant. Did you learn it at school?'

'At most schools in Poland there was compulsory Russian, but at my school there was a possibility of learning English, and both Katja and I took advantage of that.'

'Your sister is a dentist I believe.'

'Clearly Billy passes on to you everything I tell him.'

'Oh, I suspect not everything,' she said with a glance at her son who was now blushing, at the sight of which the two women laughed.

'She is an office cleaner, and she has to rise very early and work very hard to earn what is not a great amount of money. Recently she has taken to talking about the possibility of returning to Poland where she could take up her practice once again.'

'Sonja, I really would very much like to meet Marja and Katja. It's quite possible that your sister and I might have a mutually beneficial conversation. Perhaps you and your boss here could set it up, and soon. I will quickly run out of Polish dishes to cook, but I will do my best.'

'Your Bigos was superb. Thank you.'

As he showed her to her car as she left there was no kiss, but a definite touch of hands that was full of meaning. Once back inside, Billy asked his mum what she was up to?

'You now have a clearly talented and able Company Secretary, and there is no way that you would want to lose her. She's obviously very close to her sister, and if she were to return to Poland, it might be that Sonja would feel a strong pull to go with her. It's also indefensible that a trained dentist has to work as an office cleaner because she cannot afford the one extra year has to do, but probably does not actually need, to become qualified here. You and I, Billy, are, as you know, very wealthy people. Your wealth is almost totally tied up in the business – that is when the employees are not stealing it — but mine is not. With very little effort my stockbroker can dispose of some investments, allowing me to pay for Katja to complete her qualification. I really would feel it was good use of all that money.'

Billy invited Sonja into his office at coffee break the following morning, and set out before her all that Helen had in mind.

'You know your sister. How do you think she will receive this?'

'Katja's more religious than me, though that is not difficult.' Giggle. 'I expect she will see it as God's gift to her. She would not turn it down if you feared she might, and she will certainly be more than a little grateful to your mum. Indeed she will have a friend for life. May I telephone her and tell her?'

'You're the Company Secretary, you can do as you like though it might be wiser to have the conversation in Polish.'

'Of course. At home we try to speak in English all the time for the sake of Marja, so it will be good practice to remind ourselves of our native tongue.'

At lunchtime Billy caught a brief glimpse of Sonja's car leaving the car park and wondered where she might be going. The most obvious place was home to see Katja but if that had been the case she would have turned right out of the entrance whereas she had turned left. Oh well, there would definitely be reason in it. He was however delighted to see that Hugh was in and he sought him out and invited him into his office to share lunch.

'It's ironic, Hugh, that now we work in the same place I see less of you than I did before and I greatly miss our conversations.'

'On the other hand I don't miss the context in which we held those conversations, nor the house which was way beyond our means to maintain properly. Veronica and the children are really happy where we are,' said Hugh.

'What do you do on Sunday mornings, if I might ask?'

'I cut the grass, we go out for picnics and usually wash the car. You know, the things that normal people do on a Sunday morning.'

'Do you have any sort of relationship with

the church?'

'Locally, not at all. Veronica doesn't miss it any more than I do, and now our children are getting a bit older she's talking about going back to work, possibly at the University. She is a biochemist and a very good one, so that's really possible.'

'And have your former employers being sympathetic and supportive?'

'I think they've been greatly embarrassed by me and therefore not known how to respond to the reasons I've given for leaving. Maybe I expected too much, but it would have been nice to see a bishop call round and wish us well, or even write to us and wish us well, but when a priest leaves the church because he doesn't believe in God any more, I suspect it shakes them to the core. I've got over it and I'm discovering that secular employers, meaning you, treat your staff infinitely better.'

'Do you miss anything about your previous work?'

'I'm afraid not, and it makes me realise I shouldn't have done it from the very beginning.'

'But you must have done a lot of good on the way — look at how you've cared for us as a family.'

'I'm very uneasy about the "doing good" bit. It's not unlike visiting a bank robber in prison, and saying that you're sure he must also have done a lot of good in his life, you know, helping lame dogs over a stile. If I'd wanted to do that I suppose

I could have been a social worker, but I became a priest to think and speak about what is true or otherwise, to challenge and inspire. What I discovered was that most people didn't want to know about the "otherwise" and indeed, quite the opposite. That for me destroyed the possibility of real encounter. The county set just wanted me as their personal chaplain, to perform their daughter's weddings and keep alive the Book of Common Prayer. My new job is completely different. I deal with people as they really are and I seek to be of use to them in the best way possible, regardless of their beliefs.'

'Changing the subject, there is another matter I need to talk to about. You are the personnel manager and I may be your boss, but I'm also one of your personnel. Only you and my mum, and possibly some nosy parkers in the village, know that every day I walk up the lane from home to Anita's grave. Sometimes I stay there a long time talking with her — never normally to Gerald — and I have begun to wonder whether there isn't something wrong with me.'

'Have you ever heard of Elizabeth Kubler-Ross?'

'No. Should I?'

'Probably not. She's a Swiss-American psychiatrist who has made a specialism of working with the dying and bereaved. She's written a highly influential book, I think it's a great book, called "On Death and Dying", in which she sets out what she calls the five stages of grief, stages we have to pass through either as we face the reality of death ourselves, or are the ones bereaved. I think it was probably my failing, Billy, that I did not raise this with you before now, when I was vicar, but it's difficult to do so knowing how emotionally attached you were, and still are, to Anita. I have a copy of that book which I would happily let you have. It's helped my understanding times without number and often enabled me to understand what I was doing in my work. I think you might find it invaluable. If you like, I will try to remember to bring it in tomorrow.'

'The thing is Hugh, that for the first time since Anita died, the possibility of loving another person is within my orbit, and to be honest I'm very nervous about it.'

Hugh smiled and left. Billy noticed that Sonja's car had returned.

'I went to see your mother for lunch,' said Sonja. 'She invited me and wanted to know if I would be going back to Poland if Katja did? I think perhaps she's worried I will leave my job just when I am getting on top of everything.'

'And what did you say?'

'I said that there was simply no possibility whatsoever of my doing that. I want Marja brought up in this country. I have a wonderful job and good colleagues and, maybe, other reasons for wanting to remain here.'

'I am so pleased to hear it, but I feel the time

has come for you to stop hiding away your daughter and your sister.'

'Marja has heard about you of course. She's beautiful.'

'She will be if she is like her mother.'

'Considering she is a dentist, my sister also is beautiful. More than me. Perhaps you will take a fancy to her.'

'Sonja, there is only one person I have taken a fancy to, if you want to put it that way, one person who is turning my life upside down, and bringing me the sort of joy I have not known for a very long time.'

'I expect it is one of the machinists in Darlington!'

'How did you guess? It was meant to be a secret.'

They laughed together.

'I too have not known joy like this – ever, and you also have turned my life upside down from the moment I met you.'

He crossed the room to where she sat at her desk and kissed her long and hard.

Oliver's trial was drawing near and without saying a word to anyone, Billy telephoned Oliver's solicitor and asked if he could have an appointment.

'You will perhaps think it odd given the circumstances, but I would like to be a character witness on his behalf. Oliver worked very hard for my company for a very long time. He was reliable in every way and close supporter of my father. Things went wrong for him, as they might for any of us. I would like to remind the court and especially the judge that he should take that into consideration when he comes to sentence him,' said Billy.

'I must confess that it's unusual for the victim to speak on behalf of the guilty party. I will certainly speak to his barrister, who will in turn speak to the judge, and I dare say that if you give an undertaking to say what you said to me, and not to use it in any way against Oliver, it just might be acceptable.'

On the day before the trial was due, Billy received a call to say that although the circumstances were unusual, the judge was willing to allow him to speak on Oliver's behalf. Knowing that he was attending the trial, and now informed by him that he was going to be allowed to speak, Sonja asked if she could accompany him.

Oliver pleaded guilty to the charge and it was clear that the proceedings would be over quickly. Before sentencing, the judge asked if there was anyone to speak on Oliver's behalf. The first was the vicar of the parish in which Oliver lived. It was clear that he did not know Oliver very well and all he could say about him was that in general he was in favour of goodness and largely against badness. The judge had looked bored throughout, much as if he had been listening to a sermon, which in effect he had.

The judge then asked Billy to speak, but first of all warned him that he must not in any way use it to speak detrimentally of Oliver, despite being the victim of his crime, and that if he did so he would himself be guilty of contempt of court, having previously given an undertaking that he would not do so. Billy said he understood. He then more or less repeated his words spoken to the solicitor, emphasising above all Oliver's loyalty and reliability over many years.

'My Lord, for sad and complex reasons which have had their repercussions for his family, Oliver got into a mess. It was an all too human weakness that led him to do what he did and I'm sure he bitterly regrets having done it. My Lord, I earnestly hope you will not impose a custodial sentence because I cannot see what possible good it will do him or anyone else. Thank you for letting me speak.'

'Thank you for your words Mr Castle and I shall certainly reflect upon them during a brief adjournment which we will now have, before I return to court to conclude the matter.'

From the dock, Oliver held out his hands towards Billy, and said a silent thank you. 20 minutes later the judge returned and sentenced Oliver to 5 years in prison. As he was taken away, his barrister came to Billy and said that his words will have made a difference, as he was expecting a longer sentence. Oliver, he said, will only serve two and a half years. It really could have been very much worse.

'I think you were heroic,' said Sonja once they were outside. 'Will you go and visit Oliver in prison? '

'I will. And I would really like to hope in the possibility of reconciliation between him and Madeline. She doesn't care about the money – come to think of it I don't care about the money, as I never knew it was there in the first place — but I hope it's possible for them to work through whatever it was drove him to a prostitute. I'm certain that there is nothing that I can do to help them and for the next 30 months nothing much can happen, but I want to stay hopeful for them. Perhaps I should go and see Madeline again. What do you think, my darling? Would that be an unnecessary interference?'

'I so admire your care for others, but you know in this instance, it might be better for a woman to go and see her. I have a perfectly good reason for doing so, to do with Oliver's pension. That would give me a way in.'

Billy pondered for a while, then said, 'You may well be right.'

The trial was reported on the local television news and Billy's unusual character witness was mentioned. On the following morning he had not been long in his office when Daniel marched in.

'I honestly don't know, Billy, if what you did yesterday was courageous or utterly stupid, but I'm going to give you the benefit of the doubt and assume the former. Well done, though I hope future thieves will not necessarily get your vote of confidence when they come to court.'

'He's still going to be imprisoned for quite a time but it could have been a lot worse. Hopefully he'll get transferred to an open prison. He is utterly harmless after all, and he could be useful sorting out their finances. We can't have him back when he comes out, however. That would be one step too far.'

'What was the reaction of his wife when she heard the sentence?'

'She didn't attend. I suppose I can't blame her. What he did was unbelievably stupid and may well cost him his marriage. I don't know. I have seen her and understandably she is very bitter. Sonja has to go and see her anyway in relation to Oliver's pension, so we may learn something from her.'

'Billy? Is there something I should know about you and Sonja?'

'If you mean am I in love with her, and she with me, I suppose the answer is yes.'

'Clearly your luck is changing. She is gold dust and it was so clever of you to find her. I'm so pleased for both of you. Of course she's older than you.'

'Only a handful of years, though those years

have made her very wise and I can assure you she makes a superb cup of tea – for a foreigner!'

'It shows to me that you have an instinct for business. For Gerald it had become a real slog and as you probably know it was assumed by everyone that I was difficult, getting in the way, obstructing him if you like. Perhaps I did and I have to confess I was appalled when I heard that you were taking over. You were very young and had no business experience whatsoever and I really did fear for the business, but you've proved me wrong. You're doing really well and if I had one on, I'd take my hat off to you.'

'Thanks Daniel, I really appreciate what you're saying. A football manager doesn't take part in the game much, if at all, but he tries to put together a team to win the matches. That's what I'm trying to do.'

'Well, the match is going okay but before I go there's just one matter I should raise with you – no pressure you understand. You are a senior businessman in this area and I think you should be meeting others in your position. I'd like you to think about the possibility of joining the Freemasons. I believe it would help the business for you to network with others, but would serve above all as establishing your position in the business community. I should count it a privilege to nominate you and I know you would receive a very warm welcome. Anyway I'll leave it with you.'

Daniel left and as he sat at his desk, Billy almost died with laughter. He had arrived!

Ins and Outs

It was "ladies night", not at the Freemasons'
Lodge, but in Billy's own home. He was allowed
to attend provided he behaved himself. In charge
was Helen, then there was Sonja, Katya and Marja,
and last of all, Billy. The Polish food for the
evening was Baranina, which Sonja and Katja
much enjoyed, though Marja preferred the Chicken
Nuggets prepared for her by Helen, and which
Billy eyed enviously.

    After the meal, Marja went into the sitting
room to play with some of Anita's old toys, whilst
the others remained at the table with their coffees.
It was Helen who directed the conversation.

'I very much wanted to meet you Katja, because I've heard a great deal about you from your sister and because, as you know, I very much want to help you complete your registration process which would allow you to practice in England. Obviously I don't know how much this would be, but I am prepared to pay for it all. In that way I hope you will be able to remain in England and practice here.'

'To be able to register in England, I have to complete two terms of dentistry supervised by University registered dentists. The work will be totally familiar to me and I suspect most of the time no one will be watching, but it has to be done,' said Katja. 'I'm afraid that it is quite expensive but I hope that very soon I would be in a position to pay you back.'

'You will do nothing of the sort,' said Helen sternly. 'This is not a loan, but a gift. I can easily afford it and it would give me enormous pleasure to be able to do it for you.'

'I do not know how to thank you.'

'There is one way. That is to come here regularly for a Polish meal and tell me how good it is, especially when it isn't. Am I not also correct in thinking that you have no transport of your own? So, I think we should get you a car, something appropriate for a student, to enable you to get around. You won't want to live in a student hall of residence with 18-year-olds and so this will enable you to travel home each day.'

They left early to enable Marja to get to bed in relatively good time. When she and Katja had got into the car and close their doors, Sonja walked round the other side where Billy was waiting.

'What your mother is doing is truly wonderful and she is a lovely lady, but I an not stupid, and I realise that her principal motive is to keep Katja here in England rather than go back to Poland and possibly take me with her away from you. I think the time has come to tell you, Billy, that I'm never going to leave you.' They held each other tightly.

'Sonja doesn't have the words to thank you enough for what you are doing for Katja,' began Billy, 'as I don't. I think it is such a thoughtful and wonderful gift and will transform her life, and maybe she will be able to make her home here. She is very attractive and it won't be too long before she has a serious boyfriend, perhaps another dentist. But Sonja thinks there is method in your madness.'

'Oh?'

'She thinks you are fearful that Katja will disappear back to Poland and Sonja will go with her, and that you believe that we are in love and that you should do everything you can to stop that happening.'

'Am I really that transparent? Oh dear! But you are, aren't you? In love I mean?'

'My dearest mum, whom I love so much and always will, yes, we are both very much in love with one another, and she has told me that whatever her sister might do, and wherever she might go, Sonja wants to live the rest of her life with me.'

Helen threw her arms round Billy. 'I can't tell you what a thrill it is to hear those words and I will have a granddaughter immediately – what a delightful girl Marja is – and my instruction to you is to make sure you give me plenty more grandchildren.'

'Not so fast. We've only kissed a few times!'

'So what has made the difference?'

'I think it's Sonja herself. She has encouraged me to talk about Anita, and likes to go up to the grave with me, and it was almost as if Anita was saying to me "You really don't need to come any more". I shall of course. Already I love Sonja deeply but Anita will always be Anita.'

'I know that Billy and I'm sure that Sonja does too, but both you and I together have to move on and forwards. We have to. As you know, Anita and I closely resembled one another, and sometimes it must have been hard for you to look at me and see her, and whilst I'm alive that will continue, but the future is calling out to us in the names of Sonja and Marja. We could never have foreseen this and I think we should do all we can to reach out to that future.'

'I am so lucky to have you, mum. Some time ago I promised Anita that I would always look after you, and so I shall.'

They were spending all their spare time together, whether in town at Sonja's flat or with Helen in the village, always incorporating Marja in what they did. Thus far, at least, they had not spent a night together. At work one afternoon, Billy asked Ellie, Sonia's secretary if she could spare her for half an hour as there were some important things they needed to get sorted.

Greatly intrigued, Sonja eventually made her way into his office. There were questions he asked her, but she was perplexed because they were questions to which she knew he already had the answers.

'There is however one much more serious question I have to ask you and I need you to think carefully before you answer: would be willing to change your name? The thing is I would like you to be known as Mrs Sonja Castle or put another way, please will you marry me?'

Sonja was overwhelmed. This was not entirely as romantic a proposal as she had envisaged, but it was entirely typical of her husband-to-be and would do very nicely and, throwing her arms around him, she shouted "Yes!". He gave both her and himself permission to leave work early in order that they could visit a jeweller in town. Sonja was now engaged and wore her ring proudly. They went to her flat and showed Marja and Katja, who, predictably had already given up her awful job, and taking Marja with them drove to Helen's who was beside herself with joy.

Within a few days, Billy asked Sonja to come and see a house for the them to live in. There was, newly on the market in the village, a house he thought she would really like. There was a village primary school and he knew Helen would love having them near, where she could care for her new granddaughter.

Sonia was shocked by the size of the house and garden.

'Surely you would only want the best for you and Marja?'

'But this would cost a fortune.'

'What matters is that it is good enough for the love of my life and our daughter, Marja and her future brothers and sisters. For better or worse, Sonja, we are not poor, and come to think of it, you know that better than I do. I have absolutely no idea how much money I've got but I suspect it's easily enough to buy this house.'

'You know, Billy, sometimes I think this is just a dream from which I will soon wake up.'

'I awoke from a long nightmare thanks to you.'

Billy knew the people selling the house and had

occasionally been inside for Christmas drinks and the like, so didn't take too much notice of the estate agent as they walked around. The most important consideration was that Sonja and Marja would be happy living here – nothing was more important than that. She kept her counsel as they inspected every nook and cranny and he wondered just what she was thinking. They took their leave and walked back up the road to Billy's house. She suddenly stopped and turned to him and said that it was the most wonderful house and she just knew how happy they would be there as a family. Billy told her to continue on to Helen's, and he quickly returned to the house in the hope of catching the estate agent and the vendors. He was in luck and he told them that he wanted to put in an offer now, and at the asking price. They accepted his offer there and then.

The next port of call was the village school. Billy had already telephoned the headteacher to say that they might be calling and she was very pleased to see them when they did so. On this occasion they had Marja with them. The head showed them round the school and they met some of the children and their teachers. It had a good reputation and they were happy with what they saw — all three of them. There and then the head offered Marja a place for the beginning of the next term.

The final visit, made just by the two of them, was

to see the new vicar, who sadly no longer lived in the village, parishes having been amalgamated after Hugh's departure. He was younger than Hugh and large and jolly, almost a caricature of an eccentric English vicar. They warmed to him immediately and from nowhere he produced three glasses of dry sherry. They chatted for ages before they finally got down to making arrangements.

'I don't suppose either or both of you are baptised and confirmed?'

'We both are both,' said Sonja.

'The age of miracles is not over! That's truly amazing. Usually when I ask couples that question they look at me blankly. Strictly speaking we're not supposed to marry anyone if they're not baptised and confirmed, but if that was the case we would marry hardly anyone, the exception being you two.'

'Neither of us have any proof — no certificates or anything.'

'Oh, don't worry about that.'

They completed the application forms, though Billy resented the fact that he had to include his birth father's name on the form. For sometime since he had been Billy Castle by deed poll and how he wished he could have named Gerald as his father, but it was not to be so. They discussed hymns, which neither of them wanted, and music, and readings which they left to the discretion of the vicar. To end their time together the vicar insisted on another glass of sherry all round.

As they walked back home, Billy remarked, 'I'm so glad that man is going to marry us. He's a good man and a happy man.'

'I have only met two vicars in this country, the other one being Hugh and they are both good men, and they will both be with us. I am so pleased that you asked Hugh to be your best man - what a silly name! You will be my best man.'

On the following three Sundays, Billy and Sonja joined the congregation in church to hear their banns of marriage called, something Sonja thought bizarre. The services left them remarkably non-plussed and Sonja couldn't understand why the words of the service were in an old-fashioned form of English. Neither thought they would be attending again once they were married.

Katja had reached the end of term and Helen wanted her to come and stay with them for the wedding and over the Christmas holiday. She came with two exciting pieces of news. The first was that she had scored A in all her supervised work, and that if she did that again by Easter, qualification would come through by the end of May. The second was that she had already been offered and accepted a job once she was qualified. It was in the practice in which she had been doing her registration work, and further, that she was moving in with the dentist whose practice it was when she returned from the wedding! There were screams of excitement.

The purchase of their house was now complete and they spent a lot of time going through it making decisions about decoration and furniture — of which they had none. By the time they came back from their honeymoon, everything would be ready for them.

Helen, and to some extent Billy himself, knew very little about the background of Sonja and Katja, other than they had left Poland at a time of considerable political oppression, so she asked them if they would be willing to talk about how it had been for them.

'When we were in our early teens, our father was arrested on a charge of political agitation, meaning that he had expressed opinions contrary to those of the party. He was jailed and we never saw him again, receiving only a letter informing us of his death in prison,' began Katja.

'No cause of death was given, whether illness or something more sinister. Our mother brought us up through our teens and on to university. She then died and we were on our own. We both qualified and had work, but the political situation worsened considerably and so we decided we would try to get to the west,' said Sonja.

'We lived in Krakow, where the new Pope had been Archbishop. After his election his first visit was to Poland, and during his time there, and the government could do nothing about it, he issued an invitation to the young people of Kraków to come to Rome to see him there on pilgrimage,' said Katja again.

Sonja took over again, 'By this time Marja had been born and I was desperate to get her to a much better life in the West, so we decided to apply to join the pilgrimage. Astonishingly we were accepted and so we travelled with many others by train to Rome. Government minders accompanied us the whole way and it was not easy to break away from the group of pilgrims, but with a little sexual bribery (not much, just a little, which you don't want to know about, together with the promise of more to come) we were allowed to go out by ourselves to explore the city. We had said that we were completely bored by religion and the government minders understood that only too well. The two minders were probably very nervous throughout the day but were delighted to see us return in the evening. It was a much easier matter the second time we sought leave of absence and they made the great mistake of trusting us, though of course one mustn't forget they thought there was a reward to come. We went instead to the Airport. The tickets for our journey were waiting for us at the airport, thanks to the Polish refugee organisation. By the time we landed at Heathrow, they would not as yet have thought that we had disappeared and were no doubt expecting us to return at any moment. I'm not religious at all, but thanks to the Polish Pope we are here.'

'I think they should make a film of it,' said

Helen. 'By any standards it is a remarkable story. But were you not frightened?'

'I don't think so. The real difficulty was choosing the minders we thought the most susceptible. We watched them all the way as we journeyed from home and quickly agreed on the two we thought we could use, and so it turned out. Once we were on the aeroplane it was easy. We were met at the airport and taken somewhere safe. I imagine those two young men would have had a lot of explaining to do.'

Two days before the wedding, Billy said he needed to talk to Sonja about something and they drove out to a quiet country pub and ordered some lunch.

'At school,' he said, 'I was worth nothing in the eyes of other boys and my teachers. None of them were interested in me and I was without friends. At home it was the same. My parents cared nothing for me either, so involved were they with their own affairs and their own affairs, if you see what I mean.'

She smiled at his little joke but did not want to interrupt.

'I was utterly worthless, utterly pointless, and I took a job that reflected that, at the bottom of the pile, cleaning out shit from animals. It was Anita who first made me feel that l had some worth, and later after she died, her mum and dad.

'But you have done much more than that, you have brought about a total transformation inside me. Because they wanted me to fulfil myself, I have always assumed that meant a university degree and Anita definitely wanted that for me. And the evening I met you, that is what I was there to discuss. But now I have met you, I don't want to do it any more, or perhaps it would be better to say that I do not need to do it any more.'

'Do you know yet what you will do. I've seen you at work and though you do it well, I know it's not the right thing for you.'

'Whatever I decide it will be a joint decision, because from Friday we shall be one.'

'I need to say something to you also, before Friday. Tonight, or sometime tomorrow before you leave me to stay with your best man overnight, I want you to go by yourself to Anita's grave, and say what you need to. I will be honest, Billy my beloved, there is still a part in me that is jealous of Anita.'

'You need not be. If I go as you have asked, and of course I shall, it will be for the last time. The book which Hugh gave me to read has helped me a great deal to see that I was stuck, badly stuck, and I had even thought that I might need skilled help to free me, a counsellor or psychotherapist. But you've done it for me, my darling. You have set me free as once you achieved freedom for yourself, Marja and Katya. Let your jealousy evaporate like water in the sun.'

Billy leant across the table and kissed his

bride-to-be, a kiss, they both agreed later, that tasted infinitely better than the pub food! Still, it was a Wednesday lunchtime in late November.

The evening rehearsal was pretty straightforward and full of laughter. Though there was no way he would ever go to church except to get married, and that went for Sonja too, they liked the vicar very much and he seemed to like them, and was especially delighted to meet Hugh, his predecessor. It was the first time that Katja had been in a non-catholic church and she was surprised by it, that it had an atmosphere she could almost recognise, that there was an altar with candles and a small statue of the Virgin Mary, which most surprised her and appalled parishioners, who had been told by Hugh in his time there that it couldn't be removed without what he called a "Faculty", a legal order. The vicar talked them through it, then led them through it, so that each knew where they had to stand, and then he rehearsed the vows they would be making two days later. They found the words adorable and compelling and at least they weren't in seventeenth century English!

On the following morning, the day before the wedding, Billy and Sonja paid a visit to the office of the solicitor in town. They knew him well, as he was the firm's solicitor. They had come to make their wills, so that in the event of anything happening to Billy, all his wealth, including the business, would pass to Sonja, Marja and any other progeny they might produce.

Much to the amusement of the two Polish sisters, Billy had now to depart and would not see Sonja until she was walking down the aisle. This they thought totally bizarre but clearly one of those strange English customs they had to observe. Billy collected his suit and the other things he needed for an overnight stay with Matthew, kissed his bride-to-be, kissed her sister and kissed his mum and left, the girls laughing throughout.

Leaving his car, he made his way towards the churchyard. He had been here for the rehearsal the previous evening and of course he would be back tomorrow. Now there was just Anita and himself. Unlike on so many, many previous visits, he found himself barely able to utter a word. He looked at the wording on the stone. Yes, he thought, I will always be her beloved Billy, but he knew she could now let him move on, and turning away, he did so, though with tears rolling down his cheeks.

There was to be no stag party. Instead, Billy, Hugh and Veronica simply chatted and watched a little television and had a couple of drinks. The wedding was due to begin at 11 o'clock and would be followed by lunch in the village hall. There would be about 35 people present, mostly members of Helen's family who would be glad to be gathering together in the church this time for a wedding and not a funeral.

Friday dawned cold but dry. It had been Billy's last night of sleeping alone and tonight, though she did not know it yet, Sonja and he would be in the honeymoon suite of a splendid hotel in Shannon, Katja having told him that her sister would not particularly appreciate a honeymoon of sun, sand and sea. Neither of them had ever been to Ireland and although they would keep well away from the disturbing troubles in the North, he had been reassured by the travel agent that there was a great deal to see and enjoy.

Things To Come

As the Aer Lingus jet began its climb from Heathrow, Mr and Mrs Castle looked back on the day. "Joyous" was the only word they could find to do it justice. When the music had played for her entrance, Billy had turned towards her as she advanced, accompanied by her sister and daughter. and thought that he had never seen anything so lovely.

The service went well, led by their friend the vicar who smiled throughout. In the end they had no hymns but delightful music as they signed the registers, and as they made their way as newlyweds back down the aisle. Helen had sat in the pew reserved for the parents of the bridegroom and although there was probably a tear in her eyes, remembering other days, it was clear how happy she was for her son and new daughter-in-law. There had been a lot of people present, mainly from the village, who having known the tragic events of the past, now came to celebrate the joyful.

An extra place was found at the reception in the village hall for Katja's dentist, Philip, whom they enjoyed meeting. He was in his late-30s and not previously married, and Sonja was delighted to be able to give him the once-over, reporting back to her sister that he had passed the test. The speeches were given by Hugh as best man, and Sonja as bride! Billy didn't think he could improve on his wife and stayed silent.

They left for home by slipping out the back door, leaving everyone to the celebration. They needed to change and be at Heathrow in good time. Alone in the house it was all they could do to stop themselves making love there and then, but they decided that doing it against the clock was not the best way for the first time, even if all the way to the airport they kept saying to each other how nice it would have been.

It was on the way to the airport that Billy told her where they were going for their honeymoon and she expressed great delight at this, having silently hoped that he wasn't intending to take her to the Costa del Sol or somewhere like it. Billy uttered a silent expression of thanks for his sister-in-law.

Being the end of November it was almost dark when they landed and took a taxi to their hotel, which did not let them down. They were very tired and decided not to change for dinner but to go as they were. Neither were great drinkers but they had a small bottle of champagne with their meal in a dining room not even half full. Nevertheless the food was very good, and they then decided on an early night, as befitting a couple on their wedding night.

They spent their days driving through some wonderful countryside, which largely they had to themselves, staying in simple country hotels and enjoying the company each evening in the local pub. It was the first time they had seen one another not working but relaxing. Sonja kept herself busy writing letters of thanks for the many wedding gifts they had received, and Billy used the opportunity to catch up on his reading, and found himself wondering why he did not do this all the time.

Sonja said to him while he was deeply immersed in the poetry of Seamus Heaney, 'A new person is emerging, a different Billy, relaxed and at peace.'

'That's because I'm married to you and we're on our honeymoon. We are in heaven.'

'I think those things too, but it's considerably more than that. I can't tell you how wonderful it is to see you totally freed from the constraints of the business. You will probably not thank me for saying this, my husband, but I think you should give it up — permanently. I think you should start living for yourself and for us, your family, Helen, Marja and me. I want your happiness and I really believe it can only come by getting out of what you never chose for yourself. I know that you are good at it but I also know you do not like it, that your boredom is getting worse.'

'Are you saying that you think I should sell the business, or just appoint a new managing director and remain as chairman of the board?'

'Castle's Curtains is a big business and you have an established place in the market, second to none. If you were to do the latter of your two options, I think you would still be taken up with its doings and especially those of a new managing director or general manager if that's what you choose to call him or her. No, my lovely husband, I think you should sell.'

'Would it sell? You would know that better than I do.'

'Yes, easily.'

'What about you? If I sell, would you remain?'

'It's a question that might well take care of itself,' she answered mysteriously and which, he left unattended.

Even honeymoons have to come to an end

and for the last 24 hours they made their way to Dublin where Sonja wanted to do some Christmas shopping and find special gifts for her supporters: Helen, Katja and Marja, before going on to the airport and flying home. The weather had been kind to them and they now looked forward to moving into their new house and setting up home.

As the aeroplane taxied to the runway, Sonja said, 'We are returning to a very large house, with many rooms. I would like to ask Helen to come and live with us. She would still be in the village and she loves family living and she really shouldn't be on her own in that house, and we could keep a watchful eye on her as she gets older.'

'You and your ideas. You are a very dangerous woman Sonia Castle, and I don't know why I've married you. It's a good job I love you. You are right – again.'

She was right about something else too. Sonja later said that she had known within her body, almost the exact moment when she had conceived. She remembered how easily she had conceived in Kiev, and it seemed to be so again, this time in Ireland.

Although a lot of the furniture was in the wrong position, the house was ready for them on their return. Marja had had a wonderful holiday with Helen and was looking forward to her new school after the Christmas break. One morning

Sonja did not go off to work as usual but stayed behind so she and Billy could put the case to Helen for coming to live with them in their new abode.

'Oh I couldn't possibly do that. You're newly married and you need to establish your own life together without an old woman like me hanging around the place. Besides which this house has so many memories for me, memories of Gerald and Anita over so many years. It would feel wrong to leave the house and let others live in it.'

'But mum,' said Sonja, using the word for the first time, 'we really want you to come and live with us and to be near your grandchildren. And you're not an old woman at all, but we do need your wisdom and understanding.'

'Mum, please come and live with us,' pleaded Billy.

'I'll think about it. . . Ok, I've thought about it. How could I possibly reject your offer after what you have both just said. Already the house feels empty and you've only been in the new house a very short time, so I accept and I do so happily. Thank you both so much.'

'That's settled then,' said Billy.

Helen put her house on the market and moved in with Sonya, Billy and Marja. There was a sort of flat at the side of the house where she could have some privacy and welcome friends for tea, an idea she thought excellent, even though her best friends were those who lived in the rest of the house!

A few days passed and Billy noticed that Sonja was not to be found at work and looking out of the window he saw that her car had gone. That was not totally unusual and when she returned he didn't remark on her absence, but that evening after Marja had gone to bed and Helen was watching television, she said she wanted to say something to him.

'I want to thank you from the bottom of my heart,' she said, 'for being such a wonderful father to Marja. She adores you, and when her sister or brother arrives in late August, that baby will love you too. I had it confirmed this morning.'

'Oh my darling that is the most wonderful news possible. You are so clever. How long have you known?'

'I believe I knew the moment it happened, in Ireland, in Donegal. Something was suddenly different. I just knew.'

They rushed through to share the news with Helen who was almost in heaven about it, and it served to confirm how right she had been to accept the invitation to come and live here. They might very well need her. They decided to wait a little before telling Marja but Sonja could not resist telephoning her sister to let her know.

Although he spoke about it only with Sonja, he had come to a decision about his future, not least in response to what she had said on their honeymoon. He did not want to be a businessman and he had come to the conclusion that he had to make a complete break, and sell the business. This was only a first step on the way to a clarity about his future but he had made his mind up. He knew full well that he would need guidance on how to do it. He wanted the best for those he employed. He also knew he had to talk to his mum about it. She had already given up her house, which had already sold, but now would be losing another pillar from the past she had shared with Gerald and Anita. He raised it over supper.

'Mum, I've made a momentous decision.'

'I very much hope it's that you've decided to sell the company,' interrupted Helen.

' How did you know that? Did Sonja tell you?'

'Billy, you have a lot to learn about your wife if you think she would have done that. Of course not. It's just that it makes total sense. You're not cut out for business and when Gerald made his will, he wasn't anticipating that he'd be dead within a short while, leaving you a terrible burden. It's greatly to your credit that you've done as well as you have. Of course it means that you have to be thinking about what it is you want to do next, but it always helps to know what you don't want to do. But what about you Sonja? What will you do?'

'The first thing I must do is teach my husband that when I say I will not tell anyone something, I will not tell anyone.'

'I'm so sorry about that my darling,' said a remorseful Billy. 'I don't include mum among the ranks of those we do not tell everything to, and I really would have been perfectly happy if you had.'

'I know and I understand, but to answer your question, mum, I am assuming that with the arrival of the baby I shall want to stop work — perhaps before then – and I'm far from sure that I shall want to return afterwards. I have an idea growing in my mind about writing a mathematics textbook. I think I would like to do that instead.'

'Oh Sonja,' said Helen, 'after such a terrible beginning, circumstance has favoured you with every opportunity of choosing to do that. I really feel that it would be best for you both to make a clean break with the business, so that as a family we are not tied up with it at all.'

One evening the doorbell rang and Billy opened the front door to find a face he knew from the past, and one that he had hoped not to see again: it was his father. Billy kept him standing on the front doorstep.

'What do you want, for I'm assuming it's not a social visit?'

'An invitation to come in would be a start. I wanted to see my son who has clearly done very well for himself from what I can see here.'

Billy felt he had little choice but to show

him into the sitting room, where his father immediately reached into his pocket for a packet of cigarettes.

'No one smokes in this house.'

At that moment Sonia appeared asking Billy who was at the door, when she saw a man she did not recognise sitting in an armchair. She could tell from the atmosphere that she would be better leaving the room and did so.

'Who was that?'

'It's actually no business of yours but in fact it was my wife.'

'Very nice too. It would have been nice to have had an invitation to the wedding.'

'You would not have been welcome, but why have you come now – I imagine you have an ulterior motive?'

'Billy, I know we weren't the best of parents and that in so many ways we failed you though we always tried to do the best, sending you to the best of schools and so on, and that you're bound to feel bitter at times, but I want to see if we can't manage a reconciliation.'

Billy smiled. 'Oh I'm sure I know why you're here. Word has reached you that you have a wealthy son, and you're in financial straits. Well, you'll get nothing from me because you deserve nothing. You may have screwed up your own business but you're not having access to mine.'

'That's very cruel, Billy, and surely family counts for something — we're all in it together.'

'You're not a member of my family. I don't know you, and I think the time has come for you to leave.'

Billy opened the door and waited and eventually his father stood and followed him into the hall towards the front door which he opened and closed behind the visitor without a further word.

Sonja was waiting for him when he returned to the sitting room.

'I heard the conversation from the kitchen and quickly realised who the man was. How on earth did he get our address?'

'Almost certainly it would have come from the Freemasons. My father used to belong and still has contacts there I imagine. Even though I have never joined and never would, they have a network and would no doubt have found my details that way. Wretched people!'

Billy was now spending most of his free time reading books on pregnancy and childbirth. This amused and delighted Sonja. They were sitting together on the sofa when Sonja kissed him and said, 'Billy, making love with you is so wonderful, but you do know it doesn't have to be every night!'

'Thank God for that,' laughed Billy, 'the routine is killing me!'

'But I'm not talking about tonight in case you were wondering!'

At work, Billy met with the board and informed them that the company was going up for sale, and that both he and Sonja would be leaving. He explained that his heart was not really in the business, that he had never wanted it in the first place, and that whilst he'd done his best in the short time he had been leading the company, he felt that others could do it far better. Unsurprisingly this news appeared to send jitters among the members of the board, but Billy also knew that these men had contacts and would seek to make fullest use of them as they sought out possible buyers. A Prospectus and Financial Statement was being prepared. At the same time he made full use of the PR firm they hired to broadcast the information about the sale in the media. He realised too that the workforce across the country needed to be reassured about their jobs and the future of the business and he asked Hugh to do the rounds and talk to employees.

Billy received a letter at work from his father. Once he had realised who it was from he was strongly tempted to put it straight into the bin, but Sonja said that he should at least read it.

Dear Billy,

How pleased I was to see you and to know that you are doing so well both in terms of your family and also in your business — perhaps you learned something from me after all.

I now realise how much of a shock it must have been to find me at your door and it would have been much easier if I had let you know that I was coming, so I fully understand your reluctance to talk with me.

I want to put to you a business proposition. Would you be willing for me to have some shares in your company? My own business has fallen on difficult times but a small number of shares in your business would help me greatly as I seek to rebuild. That would also be a good way of strengthening the family, for I want to make up for my previous failings and give you all the support I can.

Ever your father,
John Flood

'When I read it,' said Billy, 'my initial response was to laugh but really it isn't at all funny, it's pathetic.'

'I agree,' said Sonja. 'When I compare it with my father and what he did, it is a hypocritical begging letter. Will you reply?'

'No, but I shall ask Vicky to write, simply acknowledging the receipt of the letter and offering him exactly the same amount of money he gave to me when they moved away when I was 16.'

'How much was that?'

'Absolutely nothing.'

Lydia Anita

At shortly before 3 o'clock in the afternoon, in the maternity wing of the Infirmary, Sonja gave birth to a healthy baby girl. It was good to be there for birth and not death. Her waters had broken at breakfast and Billy had taken her in straightaway. The new parents were ecstatic over what they had produced.

'Have you decided the name yet?' asked Billy of his wife. 'We did agree that if it was a girl you would choose the name, and if it was a boy I would do so. It's a daughter, you must choose.'

'Provided you are happy. I would like her to be called Lydia Anita, after my mother and Anita.'

'That is the most wonderful gift to both

Helen and me — thank you, but even greater is the gift you have given me today of one who looks so much like her mother, and with all that hair!'

After a while Sonja said she needed some rest so why did Billy not go and do some telephoning, spreading the good news, and then go home for a rest himself.

He called Helen first who was so excited, and almost beyond herself when she heard the news of her granddaughter's names. Katja was apparently in the middle of doing something singularly unpleasant to one of her patients, so Billy spoke to Philip and asked him to pass on the news as soon as possible. He was delighted to do so and offered their warmest congratulations.

'I do so admire the staff at the Infirmary and what they have done for us,' Billy said to Helen when he got home. 'They are special people and I'd like to do something to say thank you. I need to go and see someone and discuss it.'

'I think that's a great idea though I should warn you that once the business is sold, you should prepare for an avalanche of begging letters. You may need a secretary.'

He took Marja in to see her new sister that evening, and was endeavouring to spend as much time as he could with her, taking her to school each day before going to work and trying to spend time with her after school though in that there was a rival in the form of her granny.

Shortly after Lydia's birth, and when a glass of celebration champagne had been drunk by all present, Billy met with the board to discuss a takeover bid that had been made. Technically, because it was a matter of a buyout of Billy's shares, the decision lay with him alone. Matthew had already told him that it was a very good offer, and unlikely to be bettered, but Billy was not prepared to go ahead until he had had the opportunity to talk it over with his fellow directors. They sought, and largely received, assurances that the new major shareholders would largely keep in place the current staff and board of directors, at least for the time being, which is as much as any would-be buyer could say. They discussed it at length, Billy saying very little but listening intently. They were clearly uneasy but Billy thought that would do them no harm as he had probably given them an easier life, and they knew it. Without him, and more especially without Sonja, things might be very different, though they had already appointed a new Company Secretary who seemed very able.

There was no decision for them to make — that belonged totally to Billy, and they knew it but he felt, all things considered, that if he accepted the offer, they would not be too unhappy. He therefore said to them that he would accept the offer, and thanked them for what they did for the company and for all that they had done for him, adding that he knew all too well that it wasn't him they would be missing but his wife!

Daniel came down from the board room to see him after the meeting. 'I think you're making the right decision Billy. I have known for some time that your heart really isn't in it and I greatly admire the way you tackled it from the beginning and given it your all, not unsuccessfully either, but perhaps it came at the wrong time. So what are you going to do? Have you decided anything?'

'I suppose I could always ask for my old job back, doing what Hugh does as personnel manager. I really enjoyed that and before I go I'll certainly do the rounds of everyone and thank them for all their support, but no, I've no real idea what I'm going to do next.'

'With this offer you will become a very wealthy man, and I mean seriously wealthy.'

'Yes, and the begging letters have already come in. I do have one idea, I suppose – to make a gift to the Infirmary. It's played a big part in my life in recent years with the climax being Lydia's birth. I want to do something for them. That would be a good use of money.'

Billy made an arrangement to visit Oliver. He was shocked by what he found. Almost overnight he had become an old man with a lined face and white hair. He even wondered if he might have passed him in the street.

'It's pretty grim in here,' volunteered Oliver,

'but thanks to your words at the trial I shall hopefully be here considerably less than I might have otherwise have been. You were a true friend, Billy, even though it was you I was thieving from.'

'The huge irony, Oliver, as I am sure you knew, was that I had no idea that the No 3 account even existed. Had Matthew not looked when I took over, you might have got away with it for a lot longer.'

'And all for that woman. In the cold light of day I can't believe I was so stupid, though I know I'm not the first man to make a total fool of myself over a woman. The thing is, of course, it was she who made a fool of me.'

'Are you having any contact with with Madeline at all?'

'No. She wrote making it clear we were finished, and a divorce is pending.'

'I'm sorry.'

'To be honest, things were deteriorating between us, and perhaps that's why I began to look elsewhere.'

'Are you doing any work in here?'

'I'm doing a course in electronics, believe it or not. I can't imagine that with my record anyone would want to employ me in a management capacity, so let's hope this comes to something I can use when I get out – like robbing electric meters!'

They both laughed.

Billy told him about his own business plans

and Oliver encouraged him.

'Mind you,' added Billy with a grin, 'if only I'd thought of the electric meter scam!'

For Christmas they invited Katja and Philip to join them. Helen asked Sonja if she wanted a traditional Polish Christmas, though she would need help in preparing it, but Sonja said they were an English family and she would prefer a typical traditional English Christmas. Billy would have his holiday break and so it would in every way be a joy. Lydia was obviously too small to appreciate Christmas but Sonja said she would like to leave her for a morning with Helen whilst she went into town and did some Christmas shopping. Helen did not need asking twice.

In February a letter arrived for Billy which Sonja assumed had come from his father. Overcoming the temptation to open it, she drew Billy's attention to it as soon as he arrived home.

'It's the same postmark, but it's not his handwriting,' he said as he opened the letter. 'It's from someone called Rose Flood, whom I presume he married. Ah, she's his widow, so he must have died. Yes, from lung cancer in January, though according to her it was above all from a broken heart caused by my having turned him away in his hour of need. She very much hopes that I will be able one day to forgive myself for what I have done, though she knows full well it would please him were I to let her have the shares in my business for which he had come to see me. She knows that I am well-off and that what she is asking is very little but it would help her rebuild her life as he had been unable to leave her anything. Finally, she enjoins me to remember the words of the commandment: honour thy father and thy mother.

Billy handed the letter to Sonja and he sat down, even before going to see Lydia which he always did first. Sonja read it and handed it back.

'Don't you think the best thing to do with this is to put it on the fire?'

'Yes I do. It was not from a broken heart that he died but from a lifetime of heavy smoking and drinking. He brought about his own demise and it had nothing to do with me, though I like the final touch, the mention of the commandment. Perhaps I could recommend her for a job with our PR company!'

Billy threw through the letter onto the fire.

All being well, and it seemed it would continue to be so, the sale of the company would go through in two days time. Billy had already made his grand tour of the outstations, accompanied by Hugh, and was actually very sad to leave so many of the people he had come to know in the past few years and so many of them seemed genuinely sad that he was leaving, not least the machinists of Darlington who presented him with clothes for Lydia. Painful though it was to depart from them he nevertheless knew that he was doing the right thing. Hugh on the other hand, had taken to his new job like a duck to water and was hoping to acquire qualifications in personnel management or, human resources as it was increasingly being called. The two friends knew that they would continue to be there for each other.

Billy had seen advertised a lecture to be given at Reading University on Darwin and Evolution, given by a biologist from Oxford University who had already achieved some measure of notoriety for his views in his first published book. For the afternoon of his last day as a businessman, he played hookey and made his way to the University. The lecture room was packed and it was clear that there were also members of the press present. He was not disappointed by what he heard. Charles Darwin and his understandings of evolution had not been taught at Billy's school and the lecturer said it was outrageous that at this stage in the twentieth century, people were growing up aknowing nothing much about Darwin, whom, he claimed, was arguably the greatest scientist of all time. The one single cause for this, he maintained, was religion and its preposterous beliefs, almost all of which could not possibly be proved.

Religion, he maintained, at this stage in

history and in this country, was like photography or painting — a hobby for people who liked that sort of thing and who wanted the apparent security of believing certain things for which there was no evidence. As had happened in the nineteenth century when Darwin first published his great works, opposition to evolution came predominantly from the churches, because it wholly undermined the argument from design which people appealed to as some sort of proof of the existence of God and which they chose to inflict on others particularly young people. The church had been all-powerful in the land for centuries, now, he said, it was an irrelevance, the mouthpiece of reactionary and unintelligent thinking.

Billy was excited by what he had heard and he felt he wanted to know more. The audience at the lecture received it enthusiastically. It might have remained for Billy merely a set of exciting thoughts had it not been for a weekend visit of Katja and Philip. A late dinner on the Friday evening was a good opportunity for them all to catch up with each other's news.

To Billy's consternation, his sister-in-law innocently asked Sonja, 'Have you chosen godparents for Lydia yet?'

'No, because we're not having her baptised. Billy and I are not believers and she can make her own mind up when she's older.'

'But that's so wrong. Our parents were not exactly good Catholics but they made sure we were baptised. How can you possibly treat Lydia in this way if you are loving parents?'

Helen intervened. 'It's very much a cultural thing. Poland is a Catholic country but increasingly this is a non-religious country. Only a tiny proportion of the population ever go to church or have their babies baptised.'

Billy could have kissed his mum, for he knew the extent to which Katja took notice of what she said, and later, in bed, Sonja expressed to Billy her total gratitude for Helen's intervention.

Katja did not share the sense of gratitude however.

On the following afternoon they all went out for a walk across the fields and into one of the nearby woods, Katja carrying her new niece in a sling across her front. Philip and Billy had gone on ahead and were deep in conversation, Philip describing to him fascinating new developments in dentistry The two sisters walked together, and once again Katja raised the subject.

'I appreciate all that Helen said last night about different cultures, but you are not English, you are Polish, and so is Lydia, named after our mother. Surely you don't want to deprive her of her birthright and deny her Polish traditions and customs.'

'Katja, Lydia will be deprived of nothing

and especially she will not be deprived of love. Lydia is British and she will be brought up entirely in British ways. I hope that one day she will be able to visit Poland, but this country is our home.'

'But surely you will be bringing her up as a Catholic?'

'You told me that since you met Philip you have not been to mass once and I never go to mass. Billy and I are not religious in any way, and we both regard it as a duty to make sure no one forces religion onto our children.'

'But you baptised Marja when we were still in Poland.'

'You know as well as me that in Poland we had to do many things to survive, and that was one of them. She does not attend morning assembly in school or have RE lessons, and Lydia and the rest will be the same. That's what we choose.'

Katja did not pursue the conversation but remained unusually quiet throughout the rest of the weekend. After she and Philip had departed on the Sunday afternoon, Sonja and Billy talked over what had happened.

'I very much hope this isn't going to be a major issue between ourselves and Katja,' said Billy. ' She was very quiet last night and this morning.'

'I know and I really don't understand it — she doesn't even go to church now. But would it be totally impossible for you if we were to go through with it, with the vicar we know? If we look on it as a social ritual, something that is part of village and rural life. Could you cope with that?'

'I would be lying in public, making affirmations I don't believe, but I daresay that if it would help keep the family together, then, if it's what you want, I will say yes, but very reluctantly.'

So it was that six weeks later on a cold Sunday afternoon there was a small family gathering in the village church, in which Lydia, held by her aunt, was handed over to the vicar and baptised. Katja, Helen and Hugh were godparents, and for Helen it was especially wonderful to hear the name of Anita spoken in the church. Although both Billy and Sonja felt that something of their integrity had been compromised, a Jewish business acquaintance of Billy's had helped consoled him, and therefore Sonja, by telling him that although he too was an atheist, he still felt it important to observe the sabbath rituals of every Friday evening in the home. Somehow or other it felt better knowing that.

Billy met with the Infirmary authorities to discuss ways in which he might make a significant contribution to the institution, not least as a way of giving thanks for all that his family had received from them and, who knows, might very well have to do so again. A few things were considered before the senior manager realised that Billy was talking big money, not just a coffee machine for visitors, no matter how welcome that might be. They met with two consultants after that and in the end settled on a new Chemotherapy Suite, for which Billy would give up to £1 million, to be named the Castle Suite. Estimates were sought and planning permission agreed, and within six months the unit would be up and running. Ironically, according to Billy's accountant, the amount he was giving as charitable giving, would be tax-free. He might even gain on the process.

Another daughter, Klara Helen, appeared before too long, and once again Sonja had the same strange experience knowing precisely when she had conceived. She loved being a mother and wanted more. Helen now had three grandchildren, all girls, though without ever saying so, she secretly wished for a boy next time.

As Luck Would Have It

Although all in the garden was rosy in terms of his family and their financial security, Billy knew all the same that he had still not found what he was looking for in terms of the meaning of his life. He even found himself wondering whether he might arrange to visit Oxford and seek out an opportunity to talk with the lecturer he had been so powerfully affected by at Reading.

Sonja said that surely the life of his family *was* the meaning of his life, and what more could he ask for than that? From a strictly biological point of view she was perfectly correct – he had come into the world to ensure the continuity of the species and had achieved it, and if Sonja had her way, which normally she did, there would be further continuity to come. But this, he knew, was not enough. Sometimes he envied Philip and Katja, who now also had a family (so far unbaptised, he noted crossly!), because they had a worthwhile profession whereas he had by accident been lifted from the gutter, and then taken from the world of commerce in which he knew he was quite useless, to a position of enormous wealth and idleness. Perhaps he now could understand and forgive the idle rich who had gone fox hunting twice a week, primarily because they had nothing else to do and it was at least fun riding your horse in the countryside, and in any case, very few, he knew, ever saw a fox being killed. They just wanted a gallop and a few fences and hedges to jump over.

Not for the first time, when Hugh called in to see him, Billy raised the matter with him.

'I'm still struggling, Hugh. Ironic isn't it? Most people would envy me hugely and yet I'm still not satisfied. Sonja thinks that our life as a family should be enough for me and that when I had a job in the business I still wasn't happy.'

'I was quite young when I first thought I should be a priest, and when we set off together, Veronica and I saw it as the beginning of a lifelong commitment in which we shared. But life is more complicated than that, as you know only too well, and only now, well away from the church and the vicarage are we beginning to realise our proper place in the world.'

'Veronica's happy at the University? '

'Definitely, and as I've just been promoted to HR Director, at long last we have an income that we can enjoy as a family – and of course all that's due to you.'

'No way. It's abundantly clear that you're excellent at the job. All I did was to recognise that from our conversations together.'

'It's a debt I shan't be able to repay, but I think Billy, you've just got to be patient though I know it's easier said than done.'

Billy looked at the clock – 2:10am. He tried hard not to wake Sonja but she was sensitive to his every move.

'Billy?' she whispered, so as not to wake up the baby, 'what is the matter?'

'I don't feel very well and I think I'm going to be sick.'

With that he bounded out of bed and the next thing Sonja heard was the sound of vomiting from their bathroom. She rose from bed and went downstairs to get him a drink and on her return he was back in bed. He took a few sips before putting the glass down.'

'What do you think it is?'

'Most likely something I've eaten, though everyone else seems to be okay. Perhaps now I've been sick it will be over. I'm so sorry to have woken you my darling.'

But it was not over, and throughout the

following day he was wanting to vomit and unable to do so, plagued by a headache that would not go away. Helen and Sonja shared their anxieties, and although he resisted to a considerable degree, they eventually persuaded him to see a doctor as soon as possible, though no appointment was available until the following morning. Billy's condition worsened throughout the night and by morning he was in no position to take himself to the doctor's. Helen insisted on staying with the children while Sonja drove Billy to the surgery.

The doctor took one look at him and said that Billy needed to be admitted to the Infirmary, and at once telephoned for an ambulance. Billy was taken into the private wing, into which once Helen had been admitted some years previously. By now he was feeling really poorly. Sonja had followed the ambulance and now sat by Billy's bed as they awaited the consultant, holding his hand and trying to persuade him to just take a sip of water but he constantly refused.

She was ushered into the visitors room when the two doctors arrived. It seemed to her that they were taking ages. Eventually one of the consultants, one of the ones who had met with Billy to discuss the inauguration of the Castle Suite, indicated to her that they had finished and she could go to see Billy.

'They've given me something for the headaches and an injection for the sickness, but they've exhausted me with so many questions.'

'Do they have any idea what it might be?' asked Sonja hesitantly.

'They are going to run a series of tests later this afternoon which should produce results by tomorrow morning, but they think it's something called non-Hodgkins Lymphoma, which from what they say is as bad as it sounds. It's a type of blood cancer.'

'And if it is what they think it is, what then?'

'If it is, and they did say it was very unusual in someone as young as me, the outlook is not particularly good and I will have to undergo extensive treatment and almost certainly lose my hair.'

'But you will get better?'

'My beautiful lovely Sonja, I will fight this with every single ounce of my body, because what I want more than anything else in this world is to be with you and the girls. I did ask him if I was going to die and he gave me a long answer at the end of which I didn't know whether he'd said yes or no. But I refuse to die because I have far too much to live for.'

'We shall fight together and if you go bald for a while I shall knit you a hat. How's that for a promise?'

'I will hold you to it.'

'You need some sleep Billy, and I need to go for a little while. My breasts are hurting and Klara needs feeding, and Helen will need to know what is happening, but I will be back this evening. I love you so much.' She leaned forward and kissed him, her eyes already filling with the tears that would overflow when she was away from him.

Billy watched Sonja leave the ward, pained beyond his capacity to express the thought that she might be losing him and that he might well be losing his life, for he had not told her everything that the consultant has said, which was that the survival rate in one so young was very low.

He slept a little before being disturbed by a young doctor who said that he had come to perform a lumbar puncture on him. This required him to curl up whilst a long needle was inserted into his spine. It didn't hurt but he couldn't have cared less if it had, once the doctor had finished there was a porter waiting to take him somewhere for further tests, all of which seemed to take ages, but which he knew were necessary. When he got back to his bed he was having a problem with his eyes and the effect of the light on them and his neck was stiff and aching. What he needed more than anything, apart from the reappearance of Sonja, was sleep and some darkness. He reported this to the sister who brought him a mask to wear over his eyes, and eventually he found some comfort in sleep.

On her return Sonja found him asleep, so simply sat next to him holding his hand. She couldn't quite understand why he was wearing the mask but one of the nurses told her it was because he was having trouble with the light. After a while, he surfaced, removed the mask, though clearly the lights on the ward were a source of continuing difficulty to him.

'How did Helen take it?'

'To be honest Billy, she was almost hysterical. The thought of losing you after Anita and Gerald is simply too much for her to handle.'

'Yes, I feared it would be like that. Poor mum. And how are the girls?'

'They miss their daddy.'

'So they should.' He smiled at Sonia 'My darling, you do know that if the worst came to the worst, you would be very well provided for, you and the girls and Helen.'

'Billy, I'm not letting even the thought of that enter into my head. You are going to recover.'

'Thank you my love. I'm going to need all your strength to bring that about. But look I think you should go home now. You are very tired and you are a full-time mother nursing a small child as well as the others. You need at least some semblance of sleep and I'm desperate for it.'

'You need sleep more than me by the looks of you almost closing your eyes all the time, and I think you need that ridiculous mask back on again. I will telephone the ward later to find out how you are, but with an extremely heavy heart I will leave you now'

A simple kiss from each to the other said everything they needed to say.

It was about an hour later the things began to happen. The first thing Billy knew of it was that his bed was being wheeled into a side room which had blackout curtains already drawn. He was then fixed up with a drip into the back of his hand and told that a doctor would be coming to see him soon – no other word of explanation was given. The doctor who came was a registrar, one that he hadn't met before. She was very pleasant and direct.

'Mr Castle, we have just received the results of your lumbar puncture this afternoon and what it has shown is that you are suffering from meningitis. I believe the other tests you had will rule out the non-Hodgkin lymphoma which I gather was discussed with you on your arrival. You must understand that meningitis is a very serious condition and it will be necessary for you to be here for a good number of days. However, we are already pouring antibiotics into your system, and these will be renewed throughout the night and into tomorrow. We've put you in here because you are clearly photophobic, that is you can't abide the light, and it will also be much quieter for you.'

'Thank you Doctor, I really appreciate all that you're doing for me. How and when will you know how serious it is?'

'I gather you had to wait 24-hour is to see your GP – that was not good and you should really have come to hospital straight away, but you're here now. It's not as potentially fatal as the other condition, you will be pleased to know, but it can have serious long-term consequences. It's probably not right for a doctor to say it because we use modern science all the time, but we will be keeping our fingers crossed for you. I have spoken to your consultant at home and he's greatly relieved that his initial diagnosis was probably incorrect. He pointed out that it was therefore now unlikely you will get the chance to be a patient in the Castle Suite after all. Now I will leave you and plunge you into total darkness. I'll be looking in on you in the night but hopefully won't wake you up. Any questions?'

'I've probably got 83 but they can all wait apart from one. Will anyone be telephoning my wife to let her know the developments?'

'I think it would be best if I did it myself, then I know it's done. I am however, and you won't like this, going to ask her not to come and see you tomorrow. It's not because you're infectious or anything but you urgently need rest, protection from the light and no disturbance other than from pesky doctors and nurses.'

'She won't like that, but tell her from me that she has to do it, not that she ever takes any notice of me when I tell her to do something.'

With the doctor gone and the room in almost complete darkness Billy concentrated on doing absolutely nothing, clearing his mind even of his oh so beloved family, at least for one night. He couldn't face food and drink, so a little later the night nurses put up a saline drip to maintain his liquid levels, though Billy was totally unaware of them doing so.

Because he was in total darkness, when he woke up he had no idea of what time of day or night it was. He thought his headache was slightly improved and his neck a little less stiff, but he still felt pretty wretched, and he hoped that when the consultant came he would be able to ascertain from him a possible prognosis.

He still couldn't face food and he knew that his day would consist of nothing more than lying there in bed, hopefully sleeping some of the time so that the next day might come more quickly and with it, Sonja. She had obviously telephoned quite often, including apparently in the middle of the night, when she had probably been feeding Klara, to find out how he was and to tell him via the nurses how much she loved him.

'The results from the tests we did yesterday afternoon have come back,' said Billy's consultant, 'and are, thankfully, negative. You have meningitis, and, as result of further tests I think we can safely say it's not the worst kind, which is excellent news. I would say that you have a good chance of making a full recovery, and I'm sorry if we frightened you with our initial diagnosis before we did the tests. The symptoms are quite similar. We will leave you in this room for another 24 hours I think — you're not missing anything outside, it's cold and rainy, and then move you back onto the ward, by which time we will have finished with the antibiotics and, who knows, you may soon be able to go home. You done a lot for this hospital; I'd like to hope that when you leave, we've been able to do a lot for you.'

Billy decided that consultants didn't engage in conversation so much as make speeches, though he did feel this one had been unwise, verging on the foolish, to have informed him of what he thought was the diagnosis even before any tests had begun, and frightening the living daylights out of him. He thought back to his previous experience of a consultant, and the part he had inadvertently played in the suicide of Gerald.

The day dragged. As his headache improved hour by hour he began to fret increasingly about those at home. How much did they know, for example? And he knew he would have to wait until the following day, when Sonja would be allowed back into see him, to answer such questions. There was of course the telephone trolly which he could have used to call her but he just did not feel that he had the energy to do so.

By evening however, he felt he couldn't wait a minute longer before being in touch. He pressed his buzzer, the first time done so since admission, and asked the nurse who came if she would kindly bring the telephone. Then he discovered he had no money. That was an irony and a half! He was, however, able to call the operator and reverse the charges. The call was answered by Marja.

'Oh daddy, when are you coming home?'

'Very soon my darling, and how was school today?'

'Don't be silly daddy, it's Saturday.'

'Of course it is. Is mummy there?'

'She's feeding Klara, I think, no, she's coming down the stairs. It's daddy,' he heard her shout.

'Oh Billy, how wonderful, how are you? I'm absolutely desperate to see you and I shall be in first thing in the morning even if I have to bring Klara in with me.'

'I've missed you so much Sonja and when I heard what they said at first, the thought of losing you was terrible beyond description, but I don't know whether you have heard anything from here, but they say I have meningitis and it seems likely that you will not be turning into a wealthy widow after all.'

'Do not say such things. I told you from the beginning you were going to overcome this. But we did know because your doctor telephoned and informed us, and we feel so relieved, especially Helen. They also said you were to take it easy for quite some time after you come out and I will enforce that.'

'Did they also tell you, however, that my treatment plan requires lots of sex?'

'You are a wicked man, though I dare say it

might be arranged!'

'Oh yes, very important.'

'I can tell you are feeling better — are you?'

'Talking to you, of course I am, but I'm still in a totally dark room attached to a drip and barely eating anything but at least I can now drink. The headaches are more intermittent but sometimes I still don't feel particularly well and I realise it will take some time to completely get over this. I have to undergo another lumbar puncture sometime but I don't yet know when they will let me come home, though the consultant said it wouldn't be too long.'

'My darling you must rest now, and I will see you first thing in the morning.'

'I know it sounds ridiculous thing to say but I'm wholly without any money and I had to reverse charges for this call, and come to think of it, Marja did really well when she answered it, she is quickly growing up, oh how I love her. Okay, now I can rest better having spoken to you and heard your lovely, lovely voice. Sleep well all of you, and I can't wait for morning. Love you.'

'And you.'

Crumbling Foundations

Having slept so much over the past few days Billy
lay awake long into the night. As with Helen, but
unlike Gerald and Anita, he had escaped death —
this time. It heightened in him the sense of urgency
with regard to his future. Outwardly, he had
everything that anyone could wish for, plus the
more important things that money cannot provide.
But he was still a young man and he didn't think it
simply arrogance, but he wanted to make a mark
on the world, though he knew he had already done
much in terms of Sonja and his three daughters
(though she had plans for more).

A nurse had crept into his room and finding
him awake offered to make him a cup of tea which

was more than welcome. He smiled when he recalled that this was how he and Sonja had come together.

Billy and the nurse chatted for ages. Apparently the ward was half empty or half full depending on one's mood and remarkably quiet, so she was pleased to have the chance to talk with Billy.

'Do you work nights regularly? asked Billy.

'In a sense, yes, in that every third week is night duty.'

'That must be pretty demanding.'

'It's not too bad. My two kids are both at school and my husband at work, so it isn't too difficult to catch up on sleep.'

'And do you enjoy your work?'

'It can be very fulfilling, and like all jobs it can be very tedious, and sometimes it's horrible.'

'Horrible?'

'I was on duty when you came in last week though you won't remember me, and when the boss told us what he thought you had, that was horrible, because our assumption was, and and I'm pretty certain it was his too, that you were going to die – someone so young and with a young family. Happily for you, for them and for us, you got away with it. Sadly, in here people don't always do that.'

'Yes, I know that only too well.'

'So what are you going to do with your freedom now that you've escaped? You've already generously donated the Castle Chemotherapy Suite

– what next?'

'It's a very difficult question. I find myself sitting on a fortune and I feel I need to put it to good use, to do something worthwhile with it. I receive a lot of begging letters, almost every day, from individuals and organisations, and my PA and I go through them all but individual charity is not the answer. Even the Bible says that you will always have the poor with you.'

'I didn't know you were religious.'

Billy laughed. 'Neither did I and indeed am not. What about you?'

'No interest. I've been to church services of course, usually at Christmas with the kids which is all very nice but total fantasy and I'm not even sure we should be subjecting kids to that sort of thing.'

'I totally agree and I pulled my children out of compulsory RE lessons and assembly – bit extreme you might think, but it's something I feel strongly about.'

'Perhaps you're in a position to support others who feel the same. The church still has this ludicrous position in our society, all sorts of influence. I think you should think of a way you can help do something about it.'

'Do you know you might well have said something very important indeed, though that's not to say you don't say important things all the time, but in this case it's important for me. How ever would I thank you for that?'

'You don't have to. I only popped in to see how you were in when you were awake I thought it would be a wonderful way to deal with my boredom.' They laughed. 'And I've really enjoyed it too, but I'd better get back out there before I discover that half the patients are crying out for a bedpan.'

When she left, Billy realised he didn't even know her name. Eventually he slept.

Billy imagined that by the time he got home he would be fully recovered, fit and well, but it proved not to be so. Another six weeks would go by before he had any sense of energy and although in that time he had tried to think further about the idea that had arisen with the nurse, he largely could not manage the concentration. He was however fussed over by the monstrous regiment of women with whom he lived, and enjoyed every moment of it.

One morning when he was at last beginning to feel better, he said to Sonja, 'You know my darling that I'm constantly plagued by the question of what I meant to do with my life other than to be here for you, Helen and the girls. I know that I was never meant to be in hunt service or, for that matter, a businessman responsible for 300 employees and selling curtains. Work-wise and intellect wise I've done nothing since, other than read and be nice to people in the village.'

'Don't forget you gave all that money for

the new chemotherapy suite.'

'Yes, yes, that was something important. Do you remember some time ago now that I went to a lecture at Reading University on evolution and its place in the contemporary curriculum for children?
'

'I do, and you came back greatly enthusiastic about it.'

'Well, my thinking capacity has not been great in the past few weeks, but what I have managed is a thought about funding a centre, either in Reading or in Oxford, for science postgraduates to pursue their studies in biology and zoology in relation to the whole issue of evolution.'

'But Billy, you can't endlessly throw your money into this or that idea, and knowing you it would be a large sum of money.'

'I would need a lot of help in setting up something like this, so that the money I might give would be properly invested and release an annual income which would pay for it all. I feel it would be so much more worthwhile than giving it to that mighty host of beggars from whom I hear every day.'

'I would definitely agree with you there. But who would you need to talk to? And you must do it slowly, testing it out every step of the way. I think what you have described to me could be very important indeed and worthwhile, and it is typical of you to have thought of something like that, but all I ask is that you go slowly and with a lot of advice. And where did the idea come from?'

'From a conversation I had in the middle of the night with one of the nurses who was bored and came in for a chat. I've no idea what she's called even.'

'And did she by any chance bring you a cup of tea?'

'As a matter of fact, she did.'

Sonja shook her head slowly. 'That was very dangerous. Look what happened when someone else did that for you?'

'It was undoubtedly the best day of my life, and in any case her tea was not as good as yours.'

'And was she very pretty?'

' I don't know – we were completely in the dark!'

Vicky, Billy's PA and former secretary at Castle Curtains, was extremely resourceful in terms of finding out information, and after describing to her what he had in mind, she set out to find the best person for Billy to meet and then to arrange a meeting.

'I've set up a meeting for you with Dr Ronald Davies, who I think is the person you heard lecture at the University in Reading. I spoke to him and outlined roughly what you were thinking of and he seemed quite keen. He can see you next Tuesday at 11:00 in his college and he says he'll send some instructions by fax on how to find him.'

'Thanks Vicky, I really don't know what I

would do without you. What about today's correspondence – the usual stuff?'

'I'm afraid so, Billy, and from my reading of it there really is nothing you would want to respond to, or in your case, you would want to respond to it all, but Sonja says I'm not to allow you to.'

'Vicky, do you know, that woman is a tyrant. Which reminds me, how are you getting on with typing up her manuscript of the mathematics book.'

'It's not easy because I'm no mathematician and it's absolutely vital that she has the best proofreaders because I'm sure I'm making all sorts of errors, but at least this new word processor makes things a little easier.'

'I think we need another. For me. Not to do your work – I really couldn't do that and at the speed you type — but I want to do some writing, just a number of ideas I want to get down on paper and see where it goes from there.'

'What sort of writing?'

'Not novels or poetry or anything like that – I'm sufficiently self-aware to know that I haven't got in me what it takes to do those things – but possibly something to do with the dangers of religion, particularly with regard to children. I don't know for certain but I'd like to make a start. So, do you think you could order me a new word processor, and then offer me the help I need to make it work?'

'No problem. If I telephone now the chances are, provided they have one in stock, it will be available for collection later this afternoon, and they're really easy to operate, so you don't need to worry about that. You'll need a dot matrix printer to go with it, like mine. And Billy? Have you checked this out with you know who?'

'I thought I'd gently drop it into the conversation over lunch.'

Vicky smiled. 'Good luck.'

Billy sometimes called Sonja "the Chancellor of the Exchequer", though he hoped he meant it as a term of endearment. She understood finance and he did not — that had always been the case, even when he had been managing director of a company. It was Sonja who managed all their investments and maintained a sharp watching brief over their day-to-day finances. Although Billy was a very wealthy man, Sonja managed the cash. But this lunchtime was to be memorable for another reason.

Helen, Billy, Sonia and Klara all sat at the table and enjoyed home-made soup and sandwiches. As they ate, as casually as possible Billy said, ' I've decided I want to do some writing.'

'What sort of writing?' asked Sonja.

'Well, despite my appalling education at school, my results at higher education showed that I can write English, and that was the only subject in which I did well at school, but I want to write a book, something based on how I see the world. Even I have a perspective, and maybe others would welcome reading about it. Anyway, I want to go ahead with this and have asked Vicky to see if she can get me a word processor and teach me how to use it.'

'That sounds like a great idea Billy. Please can I pay for it as part of your birthday present?' asked his mum.

'Yes,' said Sonja, 'it sounds like something worth doing. But will you have the time to do it?'

'How do you mean?'

'Well you have this new possible departure in Oxford and a fourth baby to help look after. That's quite a lot.'

'When did you know about that?'

'When it happened as I always do, but I only had it confirmed this morning.'

Rejoicing broke out – but later, Billy got his word processor.

In bed that night Sonja and Billy continued their celebration at the good news of the new baby. Afterwards as they held each other, Sonia asked, 'I think you already know what you're intending to write about and as yet you haven't told me.'

'Why is it that I can never keep anything from you. If I ever had an affair you would know about it before I did.'

'Don't you ever dare!'

'I wouldn't ever need to. Sonja, you are everything to me. When I was ill and assuming I was going to die, the thought of never seeing you again just about broke my heart. When I was in my teens I fell in love, as you know, but what we have is 20 times more wonderful, even more than 20. I fell in love with you the moment I saw you in the canteen and each day it has got better and better.'

'I know – that's how it is for me, and you know that, and I look forward to many years together with our family, but you still haven't said what you're going to write about.'

'It's going to be about the way in which religions, all religions, take advantage of every opportunity to indoctrinate children and young people. We have chosen to withdraw our children from the possibilities of religious infection at school, and I hope to encourage others to do likewise with their own children.'

'It won't make you very popular,'

'Popularity isn't what I'm doing it for; it's what I need to do.'

'And how are you getting on with your new word processor? I saw you sneaking out this afternoon to go into town to get it. How are you managing with it?'

'Oh I haven't dared take it out of its box yet. I have to wait for Vicky.'

'You know she's in love with you?'

'Don't be ridiculous.'

'Oh, I'm not being. I mean it, and if

anything ever happened to me, there you are…, and if anything ever did happen to me she would be the number one suspect. Fortunately I need her to complete my work, so I have the opportunity to keep my eye on her, and you!'

Having made a number of forays into the wonderful world of word processors, assisted ably by Vicky, upon whom Billy now kept a careful eye, he left early on the Tuesday morning for Oxford after Vicky had insisted he take a dictaphone with him, which she said he must keep in his pocket, turned on during meetings.

He was very much looking forward to meeting Ronald Davies and he had recently read his much-publicised book on evolution. It had caused quite a furore, particularly in the churches, though in effect all he was doing was updating Darwin and he felt certain about his own book would do something similar.

'I'm so very pleased to meet you Dr Davies and I want to say how much I enjoyed your lecture at Reading University. It inspired me greatly.'

'You must call me Ron and I'll call you Billy if I may. Oxford's too stuffy for its own good sometimes especially with regard to titles, and thank you for your kind words about that lecture which was received remarkably well. Unusually there was no heckling from the creationists, which I always get when I go to America to speak, and I'm glad you were there. But please, tell me why you're here, you're delightful PA told me something, but I would welcome the opportunity to hear more.'

'By means of a strange twist of fate, I am a wealthy man. My wife understands finances and she tells me that I'm *very* wealthy but on the whole leaves it at that. At the present time the biggest call upon my finances is caused by the fact that she keeps getting pregnant – number four is on its way, I think she's planning more. But I want to use my good fortune for the benefit of others. I've already given a substantial sum to our local Infirmary for a new chemotherapy suite, but now I want to do something for those who are engaged in the work that you do – the fields of biology and zoology, particularly in relation to evolution studies.'

'May I ask what sort of sum you are thinking of, because that would make a considerable difference to what might be possible?'

'Is £2 million a reasonable sort of sum to be working with initially? You know much more about this than I do, and I need you to guide me.'

'Wow, I hadn't anticipated anything like that.'

'In my fantasies I wondered about a foundation for postgraduate scientific study, possibly here in Oxford. I suspect you will need some time to think it over, play with the idea and talk to others, but I am quite serious, and just in case you think I might be leading you on a wild goose chase, I have brought some financial papers prepared by my wife for you to see and verify that what I am saying is true.'

'Are you engaged in some sort of paid employment, as well as good works?'

'I live with my mother, my PA, my wife and all my children, and they're all female – when would I get the chance to work? Though it just so happens that I started writing a book on what I call the religious abuse of children by parents and institutions. From the very beginning we have always withdrawn our girls from any involvement with religious education or assembly. I feel very committed to this and want to pursue it in writing, but of course it may come to nothing.'

'I very much hope it doesn't. I'm totally with you and when the time comes if you want someone to read and comment on your book, I would be very happy to do so. Now, let's be very Oxford and have a pre-lunch sherry.'

Billy arrived home feeling very satisfied with the way it had gone. Waiting for him was an airmail letter, which had somehow found its way to him. It was from South Africa and even without opening it he knew that it contained news of his mother's death. As far as he was concerned he had only one mother, Helen, and this person in South Africa was nothing to him. Nevertheless, the letter asked whether he would be able to make a financial contribution towards a memorial for her in Johannesburg, and that they would be very happy to see him any time he could travel there. It was one with the visit and letter from his father: wanting something, and in both instances wanting money, but giving simply nothing in return. Nothing had changed. He tore the letter up and went to see Helen who was babysitting, very happily, while mummy was out doing some shopping. He told her about the letter.

'What I have never been able to understand about you Billy, is how it is that you are such a good and lovely person, considering your entry into the world and your first 17 years in it. These days people say that it's the environment in which they grow and live that causes people to do bad things, but no one could have had a worse start than you and look at you now.'

'But just consider all the good things that have come my way, transforming things: Anita, you and Gerald, and my wonderful Sonja and children, your grandchildren. I won't deny that there were wounds and sometimes terrible ones, but they've been healed and in that you have played a leading role. I couldn't have done any of this without you.'

Billy proved a quick learner on his word processor, or maybe Vicky was a highly able teacher, and he began his writing. Ron Davies had sent him some useful material but as yet Billy had heard nothing about the possibility of establishing the postgraduate foundation. He did however receive some news from Sonja for which he was totally unprepared:

'I've been to the ante-natal clinic this morning. The midwife checked us all, listening to our babies' heartbeats. When she reached me she seemed to take much longer, and then she stopped, looked up and smiled, before saying "They're sounding really fine".'

'They?' said Billy, hardly believing what he was hearing.

'Yes, my lovely man. Two of them. Twins.'

'That's simply splendid. Thank you my beloved Sonja. What a wonderful gift, and just in time for my birthday too. God, I do hope they're boys! I need allies.'

They stood up together and hugged one another for what felt like ages, and then went and told Helen who was beside herself with joy. She would now have five grandchildren.

Billy rose early each day to work on his writing. It was a frustrating process, especially when he looked back over what he had written and found that it did not necessarily say what he thought he had been writing, but he pressed on regardless. The more he did, the more committed he felt to the cause.

He was driving back from the library when he noticed that the traffic ahead was stationary. Beyond it he could see two riders, and then others appeared, a couple adorned in their scarlet coats. It was his old friends, the foxhounds. He got out of his car and walked forwards and from there was able to see some of the hounds in a ditch clearly "breaking up" as the hunters euphemistically called it, a fox they had either caught in the open, or used a terrier to bring out of the ground where it would have been shot. By now, none of the hounds he had known would still be alive, but he recognised some of the humans, not least Ray, who was clearly still the professional huntsman. The recognition process however was clearly only one-way as Ray gave no indication that he recognised Billy. He returned to his car and the traffic moved on and he left them behind, and not for the first time.

Sonja's pregnancy was advancing considerably faster than any possible plans for what might happen in Oxford. He and Sonja went to the Infirmary. The doctor they saw said that it was unlikely she would run the full term and that they might well have to induce at about 36 weeks. This, she said, was not unusual with twins and did not in any way indicate that there were problems, of which, as far as she could see, there were none. All the same they would be keeping a closer eye on her than she would have experienced with her previous babies.

Katja herself now had three children and none of them had been baptised. She was doing only very part-time dentistry, but still enjoying it. She and Philip had not as yet married but she sometimes mentioned the possibility to her sister.

At long last, his patience beginning to wear thin, Billy received a telephone call from Ron Davies in Oxford. He began by apologising that it had taken such a long time.

'However, I do think we are ready to go forwards, provided, that is, you are still keen.'

'There is no question of that.'

'We have an idea that we'd like to put to you, mostly along the lines you indicated to me you were interested in. We are thinking of a postgraduate living science foundation, enabling and developing study in relation to biology and zoology. Funding a chair would, we think, be a necessity, someone to lead and develop and give it real gravitas.'

'You would also need a building — either new or radically refurbished.'

'Yes, that's right.'

'I spoke to you about £2 million. What you are describing could be significantly more than that. Yes?'

'Yes — but not necessarily more for you than the 2 million. If it could be a joint enterprise, we could certainly increase the capital.'

'What you mean by a joint enterprise?'

'I been talking to the Schmelzer Institute in California. I've done a lot of work with them in the past and they're good. They would also welcome the opportunity to be established in some way in the UK. They are very interested in working with you, if you are interested in working with them.'

'And are they offering to put in more than me?'

'Yes.'

'Substantially more?'

'Initial conversations have focused on the figure of $15 million.'

'Substantially more. And if I was to withdraw my offer would they still go ahead with theirs?'

'No. They are absolutely clear about that. They don't want this to be some sort of American takeover but a genuine joint UK-US undertaking. That's really important to them as it would also be to us. And you would have joint billing with them.'

'That's not even a secondary matter, Ron.'

'Believe you me it's very much a primary concern with some sponsors, but the Institute want it to be the case, and incidentally, I hope that you might be able sometime to get out there to see them.'

'Apparently, my wife is now expecting twins, and the thought of a visit to California excites me beyond words, but I have a feeling it might go down like a lead balloon in our house.'

'You could soon have five daughters – you do realise that it is quite likely? And a wife? How do you survive?'

'And a mother who lives with us, and my PA, whom my wife tells me is in love with me – please tell me why natural selection has done this to me!'

'I think that natural selection is serving you well. Now, look, I have a provisional date for a meeting with Oxford colleagues, members of the Institute and you to see what now needs to be done and agreed. The guys from the States would like it to be here in Oxford if that suits you, otherwise we can relocate to London or somewhere else.'

'The hope is that the new foundation be located in Oxford so it makes total sense for us all to meet there. Are you talking about a single day or overnight?'

'Probably the latter because I think it will be really important to get to know each other socially as well as doing business together. You used to be in business, so I'm sure you will understand that.'

Before Ron rang off they sorted out dates and Billy was able to tell him something of how he was getting on with his book. Ron had some useful ideas which Billy welcomed.

Billy, Sonja and Helen set together in the sitting room after the children had all gone to bed and he reported to them the main elements of his conversation with Ron.

'Do you think you should increase the amount you are offering?' asked Sonja.

'I'm not at all sure that they are asking for that, and besides which I presume we don't have unlimited resources.'

'If we were to withdraw, say, a further £1 million, from our investments, we would see a cut in our annual income, but if you really thought it was worthwhile, we could manage it.'

'There is another possibility,' said Helen. 'You forget that I am a wealthy woman in my own right and thanks to Sonja's perspicacity, my considerable capital remains very healthy indeed. If you wanted to increase your offer by £1 million, or even £2 million, then I would be delighted to be associated with the name and the enterprise. Am I right, Sonja?'

'You are certainly right in theory, mum,' replied Sonja, 'but you would need to be clear that it was something you truly wanted to do.'

Before she could reply, Billy burst in, 'That's a typically generous offer, mum, but I think we are in danger of putting the cart before the horse. No one has actually said they want more, and I will really only know what's going on in full, when we get chance to meet all the partners. Gracious! This is beginning to get a bit like running a business again. Help!'

Billy felt somewhat overwhelmed at the meeting of the "partners" in Oxford. There were a couple of financial wizards present but most of the others were professional scientists and often engaged in discussions of scientific minutiae which left him baffled, even if a little impressed. He learnt very little more from the meeting than he had from Ron on the telephone, and although at first it was little more than a tiny seed, an uneasiness came over him as this seed began to grow into a strong sense that he was being made use of, that this really was an American takeover. In his hotel room he rang Sonja and voiced this concern and she told him to listen to his heart and do as Vicky had told him and make use of his dictaphone.

At their final meeting on the following morning, Billy's concerns were heightened when he realised that everyone was being particularly nice to him, if not actually patronising. It was true that he did not have a degree and that he was not a scientist, but neither was he totally stupid, and he adopted the policy of playing a straight bat to everything that was directed at him, which clearly frustrated them but about which they could do nothing as the morning strategy was obviously being nice to Billy.

The meeting broke up after lunch and Ron caught up with him before he set off for home.

'Everything all right?' he asked.

'Obviously I've got a lot to think about from our time together, but it's been very enlightening. The Americans have got it all thought out. Impressive. Anyway, I must be on my way and will be in touch before long. In the meantime thanks for all your help with the book. It's not going to win me many friends, but if it is so, I shall regard it as a success.'

They shook hands and Billy immediately turned his back and set off for wherever his car was parked, determined that Ron was not going to get him to say anything more than he wanted to.

'They patronised me, everyone was deliberately nice, and you could tell it was a deliberate strategy that they had worked out before we met together this morning. The dictaphone picked up their comments about me while I was out at the loo, and it was clear they regarded me as a country yokel who just happens to have money for them to make use of in establishing what would actually be their own foundation. I'm really quite appalled by the way they sought to butter me up providing them with a way in. The Oxford lot wanted it just as much though clearly they don't care a hoot where it comes from, as long as it comes to them.

'It has to be a joint decision, Sonja, because we are talking about your money as much as mine. I really did feel this was an important thing to do and it may well be they'll be able find some other sponsor willing to be manipulated by them, but I don't want it to be me.'

'Will you carry on writing?'

'Certainly. The two are not related.'

'Then, I agree with you wholeheartedly, my darling, and in any case, as you can see from what is in front of you, soon we shall both be very busy.'

As he lay in bed, reflecting on the previous 24 hours, Billy wondered whether his fundamental mistake had been to enter into these negotiations with Oxford, rather than, say, his local university in Reading. Not only had he never been to Oxford, he had never been to university at all and had just two A-levels. Yet, the college at which he had studied for those exams had provided him with Sonja and lots of glorious and wonderful daughters — and perhaps that was considerably more than any of the academics from here or America could claim.

On the following morning he and Vicky sat together for quite a long period trying to put together the right form of words to accompany Billy's withdrawal from the establishment of the foundation. She was particularly adept at finding the right phrases to use. Billy wanted it to be pithy but clear as to why he was feeling manipulated. He also wanted it made clear, and he would leave Vicky to find the right way of expressing it, that this was an absolute withdrawal and not open to negotiation. She worked on it, or at least various drafts, for well over an hour, before she offered Billy a final version for his approval. He signed it and it went into the post after lunch. He was to hear nothing further from Oxford.

Keep Buggering On!

As the time drew nearer, Sonja began to assume gigantic proportions. She was now being checked up on every week and the plan was still to induce her at 36 weeks. They were told that the babies were still healthy and forewarned that it was not impossible that they would be identical. A problem developed at 34 weeks, nothing too serious they were told, but would require Sonja to have total bed rest, which she hated and the children hated. Billy was now working overtime in conjunction with his mum, cooking, cleaning, shopping and endless picking up children from school or play school or nursery, and of course this was going to go on for quite some time in the future.

Billy drove her in for her usual weekly consultation. It was now 35 weeks, but the paediatrician said that the moment had come and that she would now be induced, albeit a week earlier than they would have preferred. Both Billy and Sonja were relieved.

With previous births labour had been relatively short, but this time it was not so. Indeed it was over 24 hours after the drip had been put up, that Sonja sensed that her babies were finally on their way. She was taken into the delivery suite accompanied by Billy (still not a normal happening at the time but Sonja was very persuasive) and an extremely young looking midwife. In the end they came quite quickly and the midwife did a wonderful job. Billy smiled. They were girls of course! The sisters looked out into the world and no doubt thought it was an odd place.

Sonja had breastfed all her children and was determined to do so with the twins and she rapidly acquired a methodology which allowed her to feed them at same time, which for everyone else was highly amusing to see. Mother and twins were home just three days later.

On the following afternoon, Billy said that he needed to pop into town to do some shopping, and certainly he did not tell a lie as he did do some shopping, but that was not his primary intent on going into town. Whilst Sonja had been in labour he had gone to see the paediatrician they knew and arranged a meeting for today. Billy knew that the doctor was aware that he had already funded the Castle Chemotherapy Suite, and that therefore she could trust her to take him seriously. He knew too, that Dr Elizabeth Hardaker was a much respected doctor and had helped literally hundreds of women through their pregnancy and childbirth.

'Tell me first,' she said, 'how Sonja and the twins are doing. I think you now have five daughters.'

'And four are thanks to you, and they're all well but especially the mother and the latest arrivals, whom so far she hasn't named. It's so long since she was in Poland I think she's running out of Polish girls' names. But I must tell you why I have come to see you as I'm sure you are curious.'

'A little.'

' I asked you once what you did about babies that were not well when born. You said that it all depended on the nature of the problem. Some might be kept here, you said, but otherwise they have to go to Reading. Is that correct?'

'Yes, that is still the case. We don't have an intensive care baby unit here. We have a special care baby ward but that's not the same thing.'

'May I call you Elizabeth?'

'Most people call me Beth and I'd be very happy if you did. Besides which I already call you Billy.'

'Well Beth, I fully understand that this will

have to go before endless committees and that we might all die before we get there, but Sonja and I would like to pay for the establishment of an intensive care baby unit here and all that would be involved in that, including staffing.'

'Gracious goodness me. I thought you might be coming to offer to buy some microwave ovens something for visitors to use, or more comfortable chairs, but what you are suggesting is monumental.'

'I suppose that the first thing I need to know is whether you think this is viable, not in terms of the finance – that's taken care of – but in response to asking whether this is what the hospital needs at this time.'

'It would cost a lot of money. Intensive care equipment is very expensive and we would need specialist staff, plus the refurbishment of rooms which I already have in mind. But in terms of whether there is a need, there can be no doubt and so many families would benefit from this and save them having to go to Reading all of the time. Wow, you have completely thrown me, Billy'.

'A long time ago now, someone extremely special to me, whom I deeply loved, and part of me still does, died in the Intensive Care Unit. I have long thought of some way in which I could use the things that have been made available to me, principally my wealth, to offer my thanks for all that was done for her, and my mum when she had breast cancer, and me when I had meningitis. After a lot of thought this is what I want to do. Now Beth, I have to hand it over to you. I will come and talk to anyone you tell me to, but you're the only person who can take this forward. I know what my part is and I'll do it but in reality it mostly depends on you.'

Billy waited until after the children were in bed and the twins asleep before telling Helen and Sonja what he had done.

'The fact that you have chosen the right thing, and one which I fully support, does not lessen your offence of your not having told me in advance,' complained Sonja.

' Am I allowed to plead guilty and throw myself on the mercy of the court?'

'You must not make me laugh when I am trying to be cross with you,' she giggled.

Helen clearly needed to speak. 'I can agree to this only on one condition, that this is a joint enterprise and we both pay. I haven't got that many years left I suppose and to be perfectly honest I don't need money because I live with you and because we live together. Sonja ensures that my money works for me but that means it only increases. Once upon a time you begged me to come and live with you. Now, I beg you to let me share this with you.'

It only took Beth a couple of days to get back to Billy and express to him the enthusiasm his offer had generated.

'We are wanting to set up a committee that will be responsible for taking this forward and we very much hope that you will agree to being co-opted onto it.'

'That's not a problem,' replied Billy.

'When you came to see me the other day I was thinking very much of how we might convert some rooms into the new unit, but most of those to whom I've spoken think it would be preferable to have a purpose-built unit. Unfortunately, the right place for this would take us out of the present Infirmary grounds onto land owned by the council. We would need to persuade them to let us have this land and with it permission to build, and I apologise in advance that the overwhelming preference of those with whom I've spoken is that the best person to pursue this particular negotiation is you.'

'I see. Well Beth, I'm certainly willing to give it a go. I've not had a lot of experience of dealing with people in local government, especially elected officials, but if you can find out who it is that I should see, then of course I will.'

'That's brilliant, thank you. I really think it will help. I'll find out who it is you need to see and let you know. I don't know how the community will ever be able to thank you for this, but a lot of people and a lot of lives are going to be changed by it.'

The two councillors with whom Billy met in a quiet pub (which he thought an old setting for such a meeting) were Joseph Kay and Henry Brown. Billy thought he would "oil the works" with the drinks, and let them begin to talk.

'I'm sure I speak for the whole council, Mr Castle, when I say that what you are doing for the Infirmary is wonderful and of course, you have already made a significant contribution in the cancer unit,' began Kay.

'You certainly have,' continued Brown. 'After all we none of us know if we will need to use it at sometime in the future and I'm quite convinced that this new offer you are making will result in a much needed facility for babies and their parents.'

'Why do I think I can hear a "but" coming?'

'I don't think there's any reason for your thinking that. It's all a matter of negotiation, dotting the I's, crossing the T's and so on,' said Brown'

'Okay,' said Billy, 'let's do that.'

'Like everything in local government you have to know who the key people are and how best to get them on your side to make sure you accomplish your task. There is an amazing amount of horse-trading goes on in local politics and Henry and me are well practised in the art. If we are both in full agreement, it will happen — it's as simple as that.'

'Well that's terrific.'

'Of course it is and we're both very keen. The negotiation we have to do with you concerns our fee.'

'I see,' said Billy cautiously. 'And what sort of fee are you talking about?'

'We thought something like £5000 each. Compared with what you're putting into it, that would be nothing more than a small overhead.'

'Would you be happy with that, Councillor Brown?'

'Definitely.'

'How soon are we talking about? I bank in London, Coutts, but I could probably get there by the end of the week and arrange to meet you here again, say. on Friday evening.'

'They won't think it odd you wanting that amount of cash in one go?'

'Certainly not. I bank with them because they don't ask awkward questions when I go in. As it is, when I do go in, they're all over me like a rash which considering the amount I've got in there, is no less than I expect.'

'And you're happy with the arrangement?'

'I probably make that amount in interest every two months besides which I've been in business, and many years ago when I was just a lad I remember my father telling me that "overheads" were part and parcel of the way industry functioned, so don't lose any sleep over me and I won't over £10,000. However, there's your part of the deal to consider. How do I know I will get what I'm paying for?'

'You have our word. You'll get your land and planning permission at the Council meeting next Tuesday.'

'That's great. Let's shake on it and seal it with a drink.'

'Champagne would be good,' said Kay.

Billy went to the bar and asked if they had any champagne on ice, knowing that it was highly unlikely in a dive like this, so he took back to the table two double brandies with ginger ale.

'Sorry about that – I did ask. So, same time on Friday then. I won't stay now because I have five daughters at home, a wife and a mother and those that are not asleep will be wanting to see me.'

As he walked back to his car he felt in his right hand pocket and pulled something out. It had a red light on it which showed it was working and now he turned it off. Now all he needed was to decide who to take it to.

'Is that Bob Wakeham?' he asked down the telephone, and receiving a positive reply he went on. 'This is Billy Castle — perhaps you will remember me from the Oliver Washington business some years ago at what was then my company. Well, I need your help again,' and he proceeded to describe the events of the evening to the policeman, ending with the crucial information that it was all on tape. When he had finished, Bob said to him, 'That's quite a story and the fallout is going to be incredible. However it's not really my area of expertise and responsibility. You need to talk to Detective Superintendent Alan Miller in Reading. He's no great lover of local politicians so this will probably be music to his ears. He deals with corruption and I think you'll want to hear from you soon, so I'll give you his number and ask you to phone him tonight and repeat what you've told me, and see where it goes from there. Whether it can be dealt with by Friday evening I've no idea, but Alan will give you all the guidance you need. I must say the dictaphone idea was a good one.'

Billy phoned Alan Miller at once, apologising that it was late but that he was acting under instruction from Bob Wakeham. Once again he repeated the story of the evening. Miller listened attentively and then said he would come to see Billy at home first thing in the morning.

Before the arrival of the policeman on the following morning, Vicky made a copy of the tape, as she didn't want Billy to be without what was his principal evidence, for it was certain that the police would want the tape and she feared, especially when dealing with those in local government, that it just might go missing.

When he arrived, Billy assumed that Alan Miller must have been through some rapid promotion process because he was much younger than Bob and yet his superior. Sonja later reported to Billy that he was extremely good-looking.

They sat and talked and drank coffee for

quite some time, putting together the background of the offer to build the new unit. Then they listened to the tape, the quality of which was remarkably high. As Vicky had predicted, the police officer wanted to take the tape with him together with as much detail as Billy could provide of the two councillors with whom he had met.

'There's a lot of corruption in local government, in both Labour and Conservative councils. It isn't often that we get this kind of information to enable us to do something about it relatively easily. I think they've been very silly thinking they could try it on just because you're wealthy. We have until Friday evening. First and foremost please do not go to the bank and withdraw the money.'

'I couldn't anyway. No one, even at Coutts, could withdraw that sum in cash without proper notice, besides which I don't actually bank with them, though I grant you it's not the Trustees Savings Bank either.'

'Good. The other thing is to keep me immediately in touch if either of them attempts to get in touch with you – that's really important. On the other hand I want you to behave normally with regard to the unit. If there is a meeting you have to attend, be wholly positive about your meeting with the councillors. Somehow or other word always gets back to those who want to know, and they need to think that you're keeping your word. And if they do by any chance get in touch, and they well might do so to settle their nerves, just say you're sticking to the plan you agreed the other evening. But let me know.'

When Sonja passed on her comment about his good looks after his departure he thought that she could not have seen his steely-eyed look. This was a man who meant business.

A whole day went by without Billy hearing anything from anyone. He had attended a short meeting in the morning at the Infirmary, and in obedience to Alan Miller, he reported favourably on his meeting, saying that the councillors could see no problem whatsoever. Unsurprisingly, everyone was pleased – except Billy.

On the following morning, the Thursday before they were due to meet, one of the councillors, Joe Kay telephoned Billy.

'I'm just checking up on the arrangements for tomorrow night, that they are still in place.'

'Oh yes. In fact I'm just about to set off for the bank in London. I don't like that amount of cash lying around in the house for too long. I'm sure you understand.'

'Definitely. It strikes me that if you are on your way to the bank, is it possible that you might just increase the amounts a little, to say, £7000?'

'I think that's rather pushing it, Joe. 5K is what we agreed and 5K is what you'll both get.'

'I fully understand, Billy, but I can't see you missing an extra 4K, can you? Think about it on your way into town. It really would be awful if we weren't able to convince our colleagues about the land for the new unit. You know what I mean?'

'As you say I will give it some thought as I go up to London. My only hope is that I don't get mugged on my way back. I could do with an armed guard or use Securicor. Anyway I'll think about what you've said and I'll see you tomorrow evening. Oh, one other thing, you might ring the pub today and ask them to put a bottle of bubbly on ice for us tomorrow.'

Vicky had heard the full conversation.

'It's a good thing these people don't know anything about new technology, that, for example, we record all our calls. Are you going to call Superintendent Miller now?'

Billy wondered whether her affections were being diverted from him to the policeman!

Sonja was concerned that Billy might come to harm in the pub and wanted to come with him, sitting at an adjacent table where she could keep a good eye on him, but Billy would not allow it, and was pretty sure that Alan Miller would not allow it either.

He arrived early, bought himself a drink and went to the table where they had sat at at the beginning of the week. Almost exactly on time the two councillors came in, bought themselves a drink and came over to the table. Each was carrying a bag, whereas Billy had a briefcase. As they spoke, Billy noticed that Alan Miller had come into the pub accompanied by two others. Sonja would hardly have recognised him in his "plainclothes". He and the other two men positioned themselves so that they could keep a good eye on Billy and the councillors.

'I take it you've brought the money,' said Joe.

Billy pointed to his briefcase, 'It's in here. Do you want to see it?'

'I trust you.'

'And what about your part of the deal? When will the council deliver?'

'I gather you've let it be known that it's more or less a done deal.'

'Well it is, isn't it?'

'Have you brought 7K each or 5K?'

'Well, as you said, what's an extra 4K to me, so I've brought 7K each, but that's the limit.'

'In which case I think you can rest easy. You'll get your council approval on Tuesday. Now, how are we going to handle the money? I think the best way to do it would be to go outside.'

Billy had been expecting this.

'That's much too dangerous. Were talking about £14,000 and I'm not prepared to hand it over in the street. We do it here and now – just discreetly.'

'Okay.'

Billy went to pick up his briefcase, the sign suggested by Alan Miller about the moment for their involvement had come. Billy attended to the combination on the lock and before he knew what was happening, Alan and his two friends were standing behind him. At first the councillors assumed that they were about to be robbed and tried to get up to get away, but Alan's friends were bigger and pushed them down again.

Alan spoke. 'I'm Detective Superintendent Alan Miller, this gentleman is Detective Inspector Robinson, and this is Detective Sergeant Benton. We are all from Reading CID anti-corruption squad, and you two gentlemen are, as they say on the Sweeney, nicked.'

The detective sergeant then read them the more formal caution. At that moment a number of uniformed officers entered the premises and took the two councillors away.

'Have you got the tape of tonight's conversation?'

'Yes, it's in my pocket. I'll give it to you.'

Billy travelled home and decided on the way that the world of the criminal was not one he wanted to be part of any more. All the same he was ever so glad Vicky had suggested taking two dictaphones with him, one in each pocket so that when the police took one, he still had another. Perhaps the time had come to give Vicky a pay rise or, provided Sonja was not looking, a kiss, unless, of course, she was hoping to preserve herself for Alan Miller.

'Does it all not make you feel rather pessimistic

about human nature? I mean the Oxford debacle and now this?' asked Billy's mum, as they sat together with Sonja, enjoying a late-night drink.

'Well, I suppose corruption and manipulation in public life are as old as the hills and somehow or other we have got to not allow ourselves to be so depressed by it that we are rendered incapable of action. Despite these two miscreants, I have every intention of pursuing our course of action with regard to the new baby unit. And I imagine that once this is in the news, and it will be, pretty soon I should think, the council will be even more likely to give their consent, almost being shamed into it.'

'Don't ever forget,' said Sonja, 'that even in Communist Poland, corruption and bribery were rife, so I think it's universal, something that is found wherever human beings are found.'

'And do not think I have forgotten the bribery used by my wife and her sister to get out of Rome!'

'Trust you to think of that!' They all laughed.

'Next week I have the absolute delight going back to my old school, as Vicky reminded me this morning. They've invited me to speak to the Sixth Form on a subject of my own choosing as a local celebrity who is an old boy. One thing is for certain, the invitation didn't come from anyone who knew me as a pupil there and I shall be interested to see if there are any teachers left whom

I knew, and whose life I made a misery. But in a strange way I'm really looking forward to it and according to Vicky, the source of all knowledge, I'm allowed to take my wife, so I hope, my lovely Sonja, you will come with me and see my former prison, though that's wholly dependent upon you, mum, looking after the children and babies.'

'That's what grandmas are for. I always wanted grandchildren and I've been richly rewarded with five lovelies – so far!'

'And they all absolutely adore you,' said Sonja, 'probably more than me.'

'Oh no. Your children are totally devoted to you and you should never doubt that. You are a quite superb mother.'

Billy said, ' I'm afraid I will have to interrupt the mutual admiration society. The question is, Sonja, whether you would like to go with me back to school.'

'I wouldn't miss it for the world.'

Billy never quite understood how information got into the newspapers or on television, but after the weekend the two councillors who until a couple of days earlier had thought they were onto a good thing, now found themselves at the centre of unwanted attention. They had already appeared at the magistrates court and would later appear at the Crown Court. Officials from the council were all over Billy, apologising profusely for what had happened promising that at the next council meeting permission for the new building would be agreed. Billy and the Infirmary could not have been more pleased.

On Thursday afternoon, Sonja and Billy drove into town and through the gates of his old school where he left the car in the staff car park. That felt like a real victory. As they approached the front doors, they were opened by two very smart, suited, sixth formers, who introduced themselves and led them to the headmaster's study, and then came in with them to meet the head. He was surprisingly young, though as Billy looked back perhaps the head that he had known had actually been younger than he realised at the time, when everyone over a certain age was old. Cups of tea were provided for all five of them and then the head indicated that the two young men who had met them would take them on a guided tour of the school.

  The tour took place at breakneck speed. The library Billy had known had been replaced and there had been further building work since his time, but basically the place was much as he remembered it. After the tour, the head talked about future developments at the school (and Sonja later said to Billy that she thought he was probably after money), and even the possibility that they might take girls into the sixth form. Billy smiled but did not make the headmaster aware that he had not been allowed to go into the sixth form all those years ago.

'It's a very odd experience for me, together with my wife, to be here with you this afternoon.' He looked down onto the many faces looking up in the assembly Hall. 'It is, I think, quite fortuitous that among those listening to me are none of my former teachers, whose lives I often made a misery. There were all sorts of reasons for that I needn't go into, but suffice it to say my time here was not happy and although I left with seven very ordinary O-levels, circumstances were very much against me and at 16 I was forced find somewhere to live and to do a job which was appalling and demeaning and very unpleasant. Then again, you do these things because necessity demands them of you.

'Encounters and events, come along, mostly unexpected. Some of them are wonderful and some of them are profoundly tragic, and they came to me. Funnily enough, as I look back, I have come to the realisation that even the school in which I was so unhappy taught me a great deal and gave me some resources I needed to cope with the things that have happened. It's taken me a long time to realise that.

'Fortune and misfortune are part and parcel of what it means to be human being. I am not in any way a religious person, because I think we handle the good and the bad not because of our beliefs or academic achievements or well-paid jobs, but because of the sort of people we are. Most of you, I imagine, will know Rudyard

Kipling's poem "If". It is of course a bit over the top, well perhaps lots over-the-top, but if you can read it without being totally cynical, it still has important things to say.

'Be ready for the unexpected. You never know what today will bring If you are open to its possibilities. To end, I will tell you the story of a cup of tea that changed the course of my life. Some years ago I went into a canteen for a cup of tea because I was early for a meeting. The only person there was a member of staff behind the counter. She was Polish and having to work at serving food and drink because she could not get work in accordance with her skills. She was actually a quite brilliant mathematician and highly qualified in business studies, and the following day I was in a position to offer her a job, a proper job in a business, where she excelled. And all because I was early and wanted a cup of tea. She has now almost completed a major mathematics textbook for universities and manages quite considerable sums of money in the City of London. She has also given me five daughters so far, though I live in hope of the next one being a boy, so I can send him here. I mean of course, my wife Sonja, who still makes a pretty good cup of tea, as well as beautiful babies. My final three words come from Mr Churchill. Whatever life throws at you: "Keep Buggering On".'

The response of the boys was immediate and sustained, and a number of them came forward at the end to catch a word with both Billy and Sonja. Just before they left and much to their total amazement, that headmaster asked Sonja if she would consider taking up a vacant place on the Board of Governors.

'Yes, I think that might be fun,' she said.

As they drove on their way home, with his wife congratulating Billy on his address, and he congratulating her on her new appointment, she said to him, 'You know what you said to the boys about being ready for the unexpected?'

'You mean about your being appointed as a governor?'

'Yes, that, but not only that. You see Billy, I'm pretty sure number six is on her way!'

* * *

Printed in Great Britain
by Amazon